IDTA

IDTA

The Inter-Dimensional Traveling Agency

ALEX STORM

PARTRIDGE

A Penguin Random House Company

To order additional copies of this book, contact
Toll Free 800 101 2657 (Singapore)
Toll Free 1 800 81 7340 (Malaysia)
orders.singapore@partridgepublishing.com

www.partridgepublishing.com/singapore

CONTENTS

"Take a left at the crossroads." ~Starlight Gilgalad

The end is near. You can feel yourself slipping away, quietly or violently. As the world fades away, in an instant or an eternity, you die. No, don't be afraid- open your eyes. You are standing at the bottom of a grassy hill. Stairs ascend in front of you and a glow comes from beyond that hill. The sky is dark, void of all stars. You look behind, but there is nothing. Taking a hesitant step, you place your foot on the first stair. Then another and another. Soon you have reached the top and the path stretches out before you. Follow the path, you will come to a crossroads. Ahead is a brilliant city with shining gates. To your right is a red glow with ominous black clouds. To the left is a road that goes just out of sight. At the left turn there is a sign that says *IDTA* and nothing more. You wonder at the sign. Ahead the city beckons, but you turn and take a curious step towards the sign. The words shimmer and change to *The Inter-Dimensional Traveling Agency.* Gazing down the path you take another step. Surely you could just take a quick look. As the distance to the crossroads becomes greater you start to see a gigantic building. Approaching the huge doors, you see a speaker. A tiny light is blinking softly on it as you stand there. Suddenly a plane of blue light appears from the bulb and scans over your body. The light flashes green and a voice says your name, welcoming you to IDTA. The massive doors slide open and light pours out, as well as the noise of carefree laughter. You look back. The crossroad is just visible on the horizon. You think, then decide. The doors close behind you.

Welcome to IDTA

CHAPTER 1

Starlight Gilgalad knew there was something special about her. Yeah sure, her uncle Jake always told her so, but it was more than that. She was extremely pretty, intelligent, and a natural leader, but that's where the normal traits stopped. She had smooth curly hair that hung down to the middle of her back, and a tall, slim build, but she was toned from working out. Your typical average Joe, at least by this description.

Her hair was a vibrant, bright red that looked like a blazing fire and her eyes were a brilliant, vibrant green that reminded a person of the purest emerald. But the weirdest thing was that she could change her appearance. No, not like putting on makeup, or doing her hair; but full out literally changing her hair color, eye color, skin color- you name it, at will.

She'd always known it, just like she knew she came from Planet Four, 39th galaxy, Isis dimension. Starlight thanked her uncle numerous times for telling her the location of her homeworld: She absolutely hated being left in the dark.

Jake wasn't one of those overprotective guys. He was tough enough to kick your butt and when he wanted something done, it got done. Being 34 years old and very experienced, he had trained Starlight in all types of martial arts, survival strategies, hostage situations and first aid, but he hadn't gotten around to actual weapons yet. She was definitely old enough to use them, being sixteen and all, but the problem was that all of Jake's stuff was in the other dimension, and the Portal was broken. So they were stuck on Earth until further notice.

Starlight hadn't actually seen Planet Four, seeing as she was only there for the first fifteen minutes of her life, but Jake had pictures. It looked pretty much the same as Earth, but with high-tech Ancient Greek and Roman style architecture, so it looked like the past and the future either collided or had a *really* messed up love child. But Starlight's favorite pictures were those of her Dad. Jake's brother Robert, looked just like him except for his eyes. Chocolate brown hair, really tall, muscular, looks like a ladies man, but green eyes.

Vibrant, piercing green eyes that reminded you of the purest emeralds.

Her mom and the Gilgalads had grown up together; and according to Jake, Rose was a real hero. Unfortunately she died when the hospital exploded and Robert, her father, was gunned down trying to get Starlight away, so custody fell to Jake, who grabbed her and ran from the attacking force in space.

Ten minutes later they were safe on Earth, but the attackers had smashed the Portals, so they were stuck. The funny part was that the Portal led straight to the basement of an empty, fixer-upper, one story house for sale. So Jake bought the house and they had been living there ever since.

Starlight knew a lot about outer space and dimensions, was really good with computers and had a fair grasp of magic, aka alien science; but fixing the Portal was beyond her. Every day after school she went down to the basement and tried to figure it out. Today was like most days; she just ended up glaring at the stupid, annoying, still-broken circle of metal.

She had read somewhere that if you stare hard enough at someone, they'll look your way. Apparently the Portal hadn't read that book and refused to even creak. Sighing, Starlight headed up to the kitchen.

"Hey Star, have you managed to get that pile of junk working yet?" Asked Jake, coming in the back door of the house, an eyebrow raised in question.

"No! I've replaced all the fried pieces, but it still won't boot." Grabbing herself a muffin, she sat down at the table. "So did you get that part you wanted?" Jake was inherently obsessed with old cars.

"Not yet, I have to go meet that guy from work. See you around six?"

"Ok, bring pizza. I'll probably be in my cave staring at that useless thing some more." She started down the stairs again, still munching on her muffin.

"Don't do anything stupid," he called from the top of the stairs. "And clean your room, it's a mess!"

"Bye Jake! Don't be late!" Starlight shut the basement door, shot a look at the Portal, and hopped onto the balance board. Her record of simultaneously staring, holding her breath and balancing on one leg, was three minutes and twenty-seven seconds. Hey, not blinking while getting dizzy and trying to balance on one leg is pretty hard.

An hour later, when she still hadn't broken her record and the Portal hadn't done anything, she gave up and started to do her homework. *Wishing that something would happen probably won't do anything*, she thought. Picking up her phone, she sent a text to her friend Emma.

u goin 2 the party tonight?
lol ya got date with chris u?
dont got anything else 2 do.
u need a ride?
na ill walk.

Great, a party, the redhead thought sarcastically. *Just what I need.* Jake was okay with her going to parties without asking, so long as she didn't do anything stupid like drugs and stuff. She never did, and if someone started to, then she would leave; with or without a friend. Going up to her room, she grabbed her purse and made sure her necklace was on.

Starlight had always worn a circular amulet with a bright blue stone set in the middle with strange markings on it. It was the only thing she had that her Dad used to own. She looked around the room and decided it looked alright.

Picking up a stray sock, she headed down stairs. Giving the broken Portal one last look, she picked up her phone, went back up and locked the front door.

✪ ✪ ✪

Jake was bored. The guy he was supposed to meet was sick and Starlight had probably gone to some party. With nothing else to do he picked up the pizza and went home.

When he pulled up to the house, the air felt charged with electricity. Unlocking the door, he thought, *Well Star's gone and what in the ΖΣЯϴs is making the air buzz?* The ΖΣЯϴs was every dimension, world, and universe- everything that exists. Going down the stairs, he peaked into the basement. The Portal was just sitting there as dead as ever. Weird. Turning it on didn't do anything either. Shaking his head, the brunette decided it was nothing and went outside.

✪ ✪ ✪

Something was up. The air around Starlight felt heavy and was filled with static. On top of that her necklace had started glowing. *Definitely something. The Portal!* She turned and started to run.

❂ ❂ ❂

Vum, Vum, Vum. The strange noise was coming from the house. *That's got to be the portal!* thought Jake, dashing back inside.

Slamming the door behind her, Starlight sprinted down the stairs. "Starlight!" yelled Jake over the noise. He was standing next to the Portal which wasn't doing anything. It wasn't even shaking, although the rest of the house was.

"Jake! What's going on? Is the portal working?" shouted Starlight. She stumbled over to him. Pieces of the house started to fall down around them.

"Watch out!" Jake screamed as a beam missed her by inches.

Vum, Vum, Vum, Vum. As the noise increased the entire ceiling was breaking apart.

"Jake!"

"Stay where you are!" Dodging falling debris, he made his way to her. A heavy beam fell right where he'd been standing five seconds ago, missing him by millimeters. Starlight screamed, her hair turning white.

Abruptly the shaking and noise stopped. The world seemed frozen and neither of them moved. Another beam crashed down, breaking the silence. "We need to get out of here. Are you okay?" asked Jake. He noticed her hair, slowly turning back to red. It did that sometimes when she was really scared or surprised.

"Yeah I'm- look at the Portal!" Starlight gasped.

Completely without a noise or warning, the Portal had suddenly started working. It was emitting a blue light, the sending signal. Somewhere out there on another world, maybe in another dimension, was another Portal emitting a green light, the receiving signal.

It looked comically like a movie, with a circular metal frame and a clear blue, almost gel-like, substance suspended inside. Then it started spinning and they were sucked into another plain of existence.

Chapter 2

Katie jerked awake. She hadn't meant to fall asleep. She'd been monitoring some abnormal Portal activity in sector seven. A light was flashing on the screen. The only existing Portal in the Omega dimension, Earth, 74th galaxy, was on and sending a signal.

That's not sector seven. This is not good. Not good at all, she thought, looking for the receiving Portal. There wasn't one. *No! The Darkist must be blocking it.* She looked behind her at an innocent looking Portal.

It was dangerous for her to have one in her hideout, a direct link to the Darkist. But it was only for extreme circumstances. *Well, I guess this counts.* If someone got stuck in the Portals, then they would slowly deteriorate until there was nothing left.

As far as Katie knew, there were no hostile forces on Earth, most of them being unaware that any other life existed. *They're stupid,* she thought. *Even the practically medieval worlds know more about universal dimensions. And the dimensions they do know about, they pass off as fiction. Idiots.* Grabbing her sword, she turned her Portal to receiving, overriding the Darkist's blocking signal.

The telltale green light began to glow and two shapes materialized inside.

✪ ✪ ✪

Ten seconds ago Starlight and Jake had been broken down into energy and zipped along faster than the speed of light.

Starlight was tense, her energy naturally fighting against the flow. Jake, slightly more used to Portal travel, relaxed after the initial shock. *Starlight, relax,* he thought to her. *It's easier.* With a great effort she managed to relax and found it was infinitely easier. *Thanks,* she thought. Then everything started prickling and she was solid again.

✪ ✪ ✪

Katie didn't know what to expect. The newcomers were unarmed and clearly didn't know what was going on. "Who are you and where were you going?" she demanded.

"I'm Jake and this is Starlight. We didn't mean to use a Portal. It just sucked us up and we ended up here. Where is 'here'?" asked the guy, who was apparently called Jake. "And aren't you a little young to be monitoring the Portals?"

"No!" she replied indignantly. This guy was sharp. "I'm twenty!" She was actually seventeen, but they didn't need to know that.

"Twenty?!" Exclaimed the girl, Starlight, while Jake looked bemused. "You look like you're ten! And quit pointing that little sword at us!"

"This little sword can fry your brains if you don't be careful!" She didn't like this girl and her attitude. "And if you're Darkist spies I *will* fry you!"

"Darkist? No, we've been out of the loop for a while, about sixteen years. We don't know anything."

Starlight and Jake were sitting on a ratty old couch while the girl did stuff on one of the many computer screens mounted on the walls. The room they were in was small and didn't have much floor space.

The girl was a strange sight. She had straight blonde hair down to her knees with blue highlights, and bluish-green eyes. Apart from her sword she had strangely shaped dark blue boots with yellow rims. She had a yellow double ruffle skirt, and purple bracelets.

Starlight hadn't meant to be rude but this girl was annoying her, and she *did* look like she was ten. "So the Darkist are controlling things now?" Jake asked.

"Yes, and they monitor all of the Portals. They probably know you're here right now. This is what I get for helping people. I lead the Darkist right to my door. By the way, my name's Katie."

"I'm sorry. Our Portal has been dead for years and I've got no idea why it started working now." said Jake.

"I've got no idea either. All I know is that the Darkist are blocking the Portals from transmitting, that's why it was dead. And if I hadn't opened this one, then you two would be deteriorating into nothing right now." Katie sighed. "It's my job to monitor the Portals to see if the Darkist are up to anything. I've been picking up irregular signals from sector seven. All I know is that someone's up to something and they're busy."

"Would someone tell me what this is all about?" demanded Starlight, thoroughly annoyed. "Who are the Darkist and what's their problem?"

"The Darkist are the current group intent on taking over the ZΣЯΘs, and they pretty much have, except for a few insubstantial worlds like Earth. These worlds are so far behind in everything that they don't even need to be taken over. They're worthless; they have no technology and no resources, and can't even prevent themselves from being blown up." retorted Katie. "Stupid!"

"Hey! We-"

"No Star, she's right." Jake sighed. "Most planets have their own defense systems, so that they can't be blown up."

"Then what's stopping the Darkist from blowing us up?" asked Starlight confused.

"If you just blow up a bunch of planets then the balance of the universe gets disrupted. Everything has its place, like a house. If you take out too many bricks it'll collapse," explained Jake.

"Wait," Starlight turned to Katie. "You said that Portal surveillance is your job. Who are you working for?"

"Not for the Darkist if that's what you're asking." She replied coldly.

"Hey, I didn't say that. Sorry about the whole age thing, but you really *do* look like you're ten." The redhead didn't like this girl, and her apparent lack of age.

Jake's deep blue eyes sparkled. "You two can settle your differences later. Star had a good question. Who do you work for?"

Katie frowned. "There are two opposing groups. The Rebels and the Resistance, also known as the R&R."

"Aren't they the same thing?"

"Pretty much. You just join whichever side sounds better. But the problem is they're so unorganized that they can't get anything done."

"So which one are you with?"

"Neither. Although they both think I'm with them. I'm actually resisting the Resistance and rebelling against the Rebels." Katie laughed. "I only work with them to get the resources I need." She gestured to the computers.

"So, if you're not working for anyone, why are you doing all this?" Starlight asked.

"I like to know what's going on, and this is the perfect place to hide from the Darkist." An alarm started blaring. "Or it was."

CHAPTER 3

"Hurry!" called Katie.

They were climbing down a ladder behind one of the large screens. "Why can't we just use a Portal to get out of here?" Starlight had asked, as Katie shut down her various computers.

"Because the Darkist will just follow us, and I don't *want* to get out of here," she replied.

So now they were descending into the depths of Katie's hideout with no idea where they were.

"Quick, in here!" Katie gestured to a solid wall and walked straight through.

Ok, not so solid, thought Starlight. Stepping through the wall, she saw a network of catwalks, pipes, and machines. "Whoa." It was an incredible sight, extending on and downwards for miles.

"Now that is a good place to get lost," said Jake, following Katie down another ladder.

Katie was fuming. Why had she gotten herself into this? She could've just let these two intruders deteriorate into nothing, but more likely they would have been captured by the Darkist. *We'll all be captured anyway,* she thought. *So why should I even bother going down here?*

The reason being, the small mechanical moon she hid her hideout on, was one of the only places where Ostium

Crystállum grew. It was Latin, the universal dimensional language, for Portal Crystal. It was the rarest of all materials, only growing where there had been a massive amount of energy released into a tiny confined area. Pretty much a billion supernovas in a jar.

Climbing down a final ladder, Katie stood catching her breath. "We're almost there." Not surprisingly the other two weren't even breathing hard. Katie wasn't out of shape, but it had been a long climb.

"Where are we going?" asked Starlight, stepping off the ladder.

"This way," She replied, heading off to the right. "And be careful."

Following Katie down a rickety old catwalk wasn't the problem, nor was the height. The problem was when Katie stopped at a yellow spray painted dot in the middle of the catwalk, told them to follow her, and jumped into the void below. No way was Jake going to jump to his death.

"Is she crazy?!" he asked Starlight.

"I don't know," she replied. "Don't be afraid of heights."

"I'm not!" But Starlight had already jumped off. He didn't mind spiders, and swimming in monster infested lava was fine if he had an anti-heat suit, but he hated jumping off of things.

He'd taken Starlight skydiving a few times, and he'd always stayed in the plane. Except for the time her parachute hadn't deployed. After that he let her go with her friends and stayed home, staring at his life saving medal.

Sighing, the brunette closed his eyes and jumped. After about thirty seconds that felt like thirty seconds, (he'd been counting), he found himself floating inches above another catwalk. Noticing a blue glow coming from his left, he started towards it with a feeling of being watched.

While falling, Starlight was wondering why Katie had jumped. She had obviously been going somewhere, and people don't just jump off stuff for no reason. *Well, except me,* she thought. *There's probably water or a trampoline down there.*

She slowed to a stop, hovering. *Or an anti-gravity field...*

"Are you coming?" asked Katie impatiently, walking towards a blue glow coming from around the corner.

"Yeah, wait up!" Setting down her feet, Starlight hurried after her. Rounding the corner she saw what looked like a mushroom with wings, stubby little legs, and a very angry red face. "Um..."

"What are you staring at, you red haired monster?" it said, looking thoroughly annoyed.

"Um..." she said again.

"Starlight, this is Kegan. He's a Portalshroom."

"A Portal what?"

"Shroom, you know like a..."

"Mushroom?"

"I AM NOT A MUSHROOM!" yelled Kegan. "I DO NOT LOOK LIKE A MUSHROOM, TASTE LIKE A MUSHROOM, OR SMELL LIKE A MUSHROOM!"

"It's best not to say the M-word around him," said Katie while Kegan spouted out more enraged arguments. "Kegan! Go outside and wait for Jake," she commanded. "And be quiet!"

As Kegan went back out to the catwalk grumbling about red hair and mushrooms, Starlight looked around for the source of the blue light. "Over here," called Katie.

Moving over to her, Starlight saw a cluster of four tiny blue crystals. "What are those?"

"Ostium Crystállum. Portal Crystals," explained Katie. "It's Latin, though you've probably never heard of it on your tiny planet."

"It's the scientific language on Earth, and it's not my planet! I'm from Planet Four."

"Four?" said Katie, with amazement. "You're from Four?"

"Yes... What about it? Has it been destroyed?"

"No, not at all! It's the main opposing planet against the Darkist! Man, would they like to get their hands on it! If they knew you were from Four, they would pretty much stop at nothing to capture you!" Katie looked at her, "What's your last name?"

"Gilgalad." Starlight replied. "Why?"

"Is your Dad's name Robert?"

"Yeah, how do you know?"

"I know him! He used to come work on projects with my Dad, before the Forcefield was put up around Four. I thought you and Jake looked familiar. I take it that Jake is his brother?"

"Yes, he's alive?"

"So far as I know, yes." Katie had a strange look on her face. "Did you know that he's an inventor?"

"Yeah, Jake says he was a genius and got paid a ton."

"That's true, but he also built a working prototype of a Transporter, using some centuries old blueprints he'd found. That's why the Darkist were after him. Luckily, when they attacked your planet, he'd been testing out a new invention he called a Bubbleshield."

"What'd it do?"

"It was pretty much a force field, except that it's indestructible, and selectively permeable, coded to his DNA, so he could pick what went through and what didn't. Supposedly he gave you an extra Transporter and the Bubbleshield. Do you still have them?"

"Um, I don't know what you're talking about. The only thing I have that belongs to him is this necklace." Starlight pulled it out. She now saw that the gem was the same color as the Ostium Crystállum cluster. "Is the gem made out of that stuff?" she asked pointing to the crystals.

"Yes, and it's the rarest material in all of the ΖΣЯϴs. It can only grow if there is a massive amount of energy released in a tiny space like a jar. This is one of the only clusters in undiscovered existence."

"Wow, so what's it for?"

"So far as I know, it only has one use and that's making a Transporter."

At that moment Jake walked in, followed closely by Kegan. "What is this thing?" He demanded as Kegan fluttered into his back. "He kept asking me questions! 'Are you Jake?' 'What are you doing here?' 'Why are you so tall?'"

"This is Kegan," laughed Starlight. "He's a Portalshroom."

"Whatever, did I hear someone say that someone is making a Transporter?"

"Yeah, Dad did, and it's this one." She held up the necklace again.

"So that's what it is! I knew it did something! Wow, that's useful. Now you can go wherever you want, whenever you want!" Jake said as Kegan gave him the evil eye.

"Cool, did you know that Dad's alive?"

"Um, I guess. I didn't have any proof that he was dead, so..."

"Well, you always made it sound like he died."

"Hey! I thought he did at first! You can't blame me! I guess he just tripped and lost his grip on you. You're lucky I caught you, or you'd have a broken neck!" Jake retorted.

"I hate to break up this lovely conversation," interrupted Katie. "But we need to grab the crystals and go." She slipped on a black protective glove, pried them off and stuck the hand sized cluster into a protected pocket on her skirt. "If you have any idea how to use the Transporter, now would be a good time."

Starlight frowned thinking, *it's not like there's an activation code or something.* Jake had said that Robert liked obvious stuff like passwords. What's the password? Password... *Activation code! That's it!*

She looked at the gem. Pressing her finger to it, she said, "Activation code." The gem started glowing. "Where do you want to go?" she asked the group. It was a mistake. The Transporter apparently took her question as a command and they were all gone in an instant.

✪ ✪ ✪

Starlight looked around at her new surroundings. Katie was standing next to her looking disoriented. "Jake, where are we?" There was no reply. "Jake?" Looking around her, Starlight only saw Katie. There was no sign of Jake or the Portalshroom

CHAPTER 4

Starlight was running out of ideas. They were lost in hilly terrain dotted with rocks, with a horde of bloodthirsty things surrounding them. "Katie!"

"I'm working on it!" For some reason she was sitting on the ground fiddling with her boots.

"What are you doing?" asked Starlight, exasperated, just as one of the things started talking.

"What do we have here?" It asked with a whiny voice. Turning to one of the others, it said, "They smell like humans, but I've never heard of ones that look like this."

"Who cares," one of the others replied. "Let's eat 'em!" With that it started forward, a look of desperation on its face. "STOP!" yelled Whiny. "We have orders!" He- Starlight assumed it was a he- grabbed the desperate one by the neck.

"But I'm hungry!" protested Desperate. "There's been no food for days!"

"There will be food if you don't stop your sniveling. I'll see to it personally!" threatened Whiny. "Tie them up!"

Starlight felt a hand grab her arm, "Don't touch me!" she shouted, kicking her feet.

"Hold on and stop wiggling!" Katie grunted, pulling her into the air.

"They're getting away! Stop them!" Commanded Whiny.

17

"Are you wearing...?"

"Rocket boots. Yeah, they take a while to warm up." Katie laughed. "And just in time too."

"Well, what are you waiting for? Get us out of here!"

"You're too heavy! I can't lift you any higher!" Katie struggled to keep them aloft. "We're going down!" The boosters, fighting to keep them up, failed altogether.

The two would be escapees were grabbed by unfriendly hands, tied together by their wrists, and shoved into motion by the things.

"Starlight!" hissed Katie. But she was abruptly cut off by a returning scout. "Gushbud!" he called. "There's a party of those blasted elves closing in on us!"

"Rrrahh! Get your weapons you stinking filth!" ordered Whiny/Gushbud.

Starlight heard a horn blast nearby. "Close ranks!" Gushbud shouted the order above the clatter of hooves. "Get 'em boys!"

To Katie, the next few minutes were a blur. There was a lot of screaming, yelling, hacking, and stabbing going on, with the occasional arrow flashing by. *Well this is medieval,* she thought, surprised that she hadn't been hurt yet.

"Any survivors?" Asked someone. Katie looked up from her position on the ground. "These two aren't Lerlins." *Lerlins? What the heck are Lerlins?*

"Are you two alright?" Asked a guy, who was super cute. Katie felt gentle hands untying them. "Can you stand?"

"Of course we can stand! Right Katie?" Starlight grabbed her arm and pulled her to her feet.

"Ow! What just happened?" she demanded.

"Of course they can stand! They're not hurt are they?" replied a girl with... *Are her eyes silver? Ok that's weird.*

"No, we're not hurt thank you very much. Now if you could tell us where we are?"

"Katie! Be nice!" Scolded Starlight, whispering, "I think I know where we are. Now shut up and start being polite. These people take things seriously."

I am being nice! Katie fumed silently. "Ok, if you're so smart, where are we?"

"Excuse me, but we need to get back to the valley, or we will miss the celebration. You're welcome to come with us." Invited the cute guy.

"Um, yeah, sure." Katie glanced at Starlight. "Dibs."

"Well then, dibs it is." he said, confused. "Come." Lifting Katie onto his horse, he gave an order in another language, and they started off.

Starlight was stuck riding with miss grumpy silver eyes. The first and only thing she had said was, "You keep your eyes off my brother, or I personally guarantee that you won't have any." *Harsh*, thought Starlight. *Considering that it was Katie who called dibs.*

"Don't worry he's not my type." She replied, not even getting a glance from the girl in front of her. *Whatever.*

Rounding a hill, Starlight saw a deep, steep sided canyon covered in trees with no visible way to get down. "Whoa." The party started to dismount.

Sliding off the horse, Starlight followed the silver eyed girl into a patch of trees to their left. Hurrying to catch up with Katie, she saw a boulder covered with hanging vines and creepers.

"Isn't this cool?" asked Katie excitedly.

"Easy for you to say, I got stuck with your boyfriend's over protective sister."

"That's nice, his name is Lester. I bet you there's a secret entrance somewhere!"

"Lester? That's not a..." Someone had swept the vines to one side revealing a passageway.

"Told you!" exclaimed Katie. "Come on!" Joining the single file line they passed into the dark tunnel, carefully stepping down the stairs.

"Do not worry. We will be underground for only a few yards," said Lester, leading his horse behind them.

They came out onto a ledge, the path winding down the cliffs, hidden by the green foliage and vines. *Smart, you can't even trace the path back up to the tunnel,* the redhead thought. Following the group, Starlight caught glimpses of the canyon as it widened into a valley filled with rivers and glades. As the path leveled out, the party remounted and rode for a good half an hour the rest of the way to a small patch of trees.

Rounding the final one, an amazing white bridge came into view dead ahead, spanning a fast running river. Following its path upstream, Starlight saw a series of small waterfalls running under more of the bridges. She dismounted and ran her hand over the twisting strands of white stone that made up the railings. *Wow, this is incredible!* Downstream the river winded away to form a lake at the far end where the canyon started.

"Hurry up Starlight!" called Katie, excitedly.

"I'm coming! I'm coming!" She ran, jumping up to mount behind her silent companion. She started as the girl remarked, "You've been riding before?"

"Oh, uh yeah, my uncle taught me." *So she does talk.*

"You're not trying to show off or anything right? Because I'm not impressed."

Jeez, what is with this girl? She's worse than Katie. "No! I wasn't! And I don't care if you're impressed or not. I just need to figure out how I'm going to find my uncle and then I'll get out of your hair!"

"Your uncle's lost?"

"No, yes, I don't know! We got separated getting here." Starlight wasn't someone who cried easily, but everything that had happened today was starting to have an effect. *No way am I going to let this rude, silver eyed elf make me cry!*

"I'm sorry for your loss," responded the girl, not sounding sorry at all. Starlight was about to reply when they rounded a boulder and the whole valley came into view. *Call me crazy, but that looked exactly like...*

"Rivendell!" She exclaimed.

"Rivendell?" Muttered the girl sarcastically. "Right." She steered the horse over to Katie and Lester, while the other elves unsaddled their horses.

"Welcome to Emerald Valley," said Lester.

"Wow! Starlight, look at it! It's amazing!" Katie was already dismounting and moved to a little observation area, with more of the white stone.

"I've seen it before, I think..." she responded, joining Katie. "But not like this."

"It's nice to get out my cave for a while. I've been to lots of cool places, but I've never seen anything like here!" Katie continued to express her amazement, but Starlight wasn't listening.

"The redhead's from Earth." The girl was saying to Lester.

"How do you know Arya?" He said her name like uh-rye-uh.

"She thinks this is Rivendell."

"So?"

"I'm just saying these Earth people keep popping up everywhere."

"Why's that a problem?" asked Lester.

"Because, they keep stealing ideas and things from the rest of the ZΣЯⴲs! They're a nuisance and they should just stay on their little isolated planet!" Retorted Arya.

"Oh, Come on, Arya! It's not like they can do any harm, what are they going to do? Build an army and take over the ZΣЯΘs? We've got the Darkist for that," he scoffed. "Let's go. It's almost sunset. You know they'll start without us."

Fine! This isn't Rivendell, there are those Darkist people again, and does everybody know about Earth? Starlight thought, angrily. This girl was starting to get on her nerves.

"Katie, Starlight, we must hurry or we will miss the festivities," called Lester. *Another thing,* thought Starlight. *Why does he talk like an old fashioned elf to us, but not to Arya?*

Shaking her head, she headed down the path, more like a road now, and heard music coming from a huge clearing in the middle of the Rivendell style buildings. They were greeted by two guards wearing fancy clothes. Lester and Arya swapped some chitchat with them in what Starlight assumed was Elvish, *But how should I know? This isn't Middle Earth. Or is it?* Either way, she and Katie were introduced and then were swept away by some gorgeous elves to change out of their mud and blood stained clothes.

Ten minutes later, they were cleaned up and ready to party. The party, surprisingly, was to celebrate Lester and Arya's birthday. Equally surprising was the fact that they were royalty.

"You can totally see that Lester has to be at least a lord or something," Katie was saying, sitting in front of the mirror. "But a prince? Wow. You think he likes me?"

"He liked you before you knew he was a prince, so he's probably not going to stop now." Reasoned Starlight. *I guess she's warming up to me now.* "Do you think Jake is okay? I can't stop worrying about him."

"Oh come on! He's probably on *your planet* getting reinforcements."

She said *your planet* like it was a big deal. *It probably is to her,* thought Starlight. "How would he have gotten there?"

"He probably wanted to go there, so when you said 'Where do you want to go?', the Transporter took us where we wanted to go. But come on!" She repeated. "I'm sure he's fine. We have a party to get to!" With that Katie stood up and turned in a circle, showing off her knee length, long sleeve purple dress. It sparkled as the rays from the setting sun hit her. "Let's party!"

✪ ✪ ✪

Lester sighed, wishing he could be outside enjoying the party. "Why do we have to make an entrance?" He asked Arya, as she straightened his crown.

"Because, we're royalty, and it's our party."

Frowning he moved the crown back to its original position, at a slight angle. "Yeah, but still. It's boring just sitting here." They were waiting for an attendant to come and escort them to the party. Peeking out the window, Lester saw the two newcomers had already joined the party and were surrounded by a group of girls. He watched as Katie twirled, her sparkly dress and long hair fanning out around her. *Wow. She's amazing!*

"Your highnesses," called the attendant, from the doorway. "We're ready for your appearance."

"Finally!" Muttered Lester, pulling away from the window. His sister made a move to correct his crown again, but he ducked. "Come on!"

Stepping outside after Arya, someone announced, "Her royal highness, Princess Arya Greylance. Happy 21th birthday!" She gave a quick curtsy and stepped into the crowd heading for her chair in one of the pavilions, ignoring everyone. *So much for a regal entrance,* he thought.

Determined to show her up, he winked at the announcer, who responded with, "Introducing, Lester Greylance, Prince of Parties!"

"So let's get this party started!" Scanning the crowd his eyes settled on Katie. He grinned, starting towards her. "May I have this dance?"

Blushing, she took his outstretched hand, and they headed to the dance floor.

✪ ✪ ✪

Starlight was amazed by how much this party resembled the ones back on Earth. Everyone was wearing a mix of old fashioned and relatively modern clothes. Her own dress was a bluish-green color, ending a few inches above her knees, and with only one thin strap she would have been cold except for the fuzzy little cape covering her shoulders.

Even the music was sort of similar; they had a live band playing with guitar looking things, a set of drums, and a bunch of other instruments. The only thing that was weird was that there weren't any techno sounds.

Whatever, it still sounds pretty good, she thought, clapping to something that was definitely pop. The girls around her were giggling at something. She ignored them, letting the music and smell of food surround her. "Excuse me." Someone tapped her shoulder. She opened her eyes, and saw the hottest guy she had ever seen. "May I have this dance?" He asked, holding out his hand.

"Oh! Um. Sure!" She stuttered as her hair turned dark purple.

His eyes widened, "You can Illusionate?"

"Oh, no I- Illusionate?"

"Yeah, you can change how you look at will."

"Oh. Yeah I can Illusionate, I guess, although most of the time it's unintentional."

"That's all right, my friend is an Illusionator and her hair changes color too." He laughed. Starlight relaxed, her hair turning to its original brilliance. "My name's Ben."

"Starlight." She said easily, her embarrassment gone. "Go dance already!" said one of the girls, causing a hurricane of giggles.

"Come on," Ben pulled her onto the dance floor. A slow song was playing and Starlight caught sight of Katie in the arms of Lester. Catching her eye, she smiled and waved making Katie blush. Lester said something and she giggled.

"So Starlight," started Ben. "You're new around here?"

"Yes, I'm just visiting." She glanced down at her transporter. "Sort of..."

"Sort of?" He asked. They were passing by Arya. As usual, she was glaring at Starlight. Starlight glared back.

"Who are you staring at?" Asked Ben. He looked up and saw Arya. "Oh..."

"Ben? Ben!" She yelled, angrily coming up to them. "Where have you been? WHY ARE YOU WITH HER?"

"What's her problem?" Asked Starlight.

"She," Ben said alarmed. "Is my girlfriend."

CHAPTER 5

Jake wished he could plug his ears. The stupid Portalshroom just wouldn't shut up. Unfortunately, his hands were tied behind his back at the moment. *Just my luck*, he thought. *Of course I would have to be the one who turns up into the middle of a Darkist patrol.* On top of that he was on Planet Four. So much for the no Darkist allowed rule.

He'd disappeared from Katie's hideout without warning. As soon as Jake had realized that he was alone, someone had hit him with a tranquilizer dart. After coming to, he'd been interrogated, threatened, and beaten up pretty badly. Making matters worse, Kegan kept complaining about anything he could think about. Currently he was on another mushroom rant. "I AM NOT A MUSHROOM!"

His guards were keeping themselves amused by egging him on. "Yes you are."

"NO I AM NOT!"

"Oh yeah? Then prove it!"

"Fine!" Kegan took a deep breath, preparing for his mushroom speech.

"No, please stop!" Jake moaned. One of the guards rounded on him. "Did you say something, pretty boy?" Jake held his tongue.

"Cause I think you did. Look at me when I'm talking to you!" He slammed his boot onto Jake's throat and shoved his head up. Forced to look at the guard, but being deprived of air, he stared dumbly into the other man's eyes. "You staring at me? Why you staring at me?" Demanded the guard. The pressure on Jake's throat lessened slightly, and he sucked in a breath. "You think I'm pretty? Is that it?"

"No." Jake spat the word out, shaking his head.

"Aww, that's too bad, cause I'm a pretty sort of guy." The boot pulled back and kicked him hard in the head. Stunned, Jake reeled to the side, gasping. "That's right pretty boy. You keep your mouth shut."

"Watch them!" He ordered, and walked off.

"Hey, you alright?" Asked the remaining guard. He stood with his arms crossed in front of him. "Sorry about that, Casper has major anger issues, obviously. I'm not really supposed to be talking to you, but people call me Dare."

"Nice name." Jake said when the world had stopped spinning. "Why?"

"Oh, supposedly I take a lot of risks," explained Dare shrugging. Jake expected Kegan to start talking again, but when he looked at the Portalshroom, he was fast asleep and snoring.

"He even snores like a mushroom," Jake risked the word, but Kegan didn't even twitch.

"He's kinda cute," said Dare squatting down. "Where'd you find him?" He looked around but his buddies were out scouting the area. "You look a lot like someone I know." He said, sitting down, his back to the setting sun. "Are you by any chance related to a Robert Gilgalad?"

What could it hurt? Jake thought. *I'm already in about as much trouble as I can be.* "He's my brother. And I was actually coming to look for him." It wasn't a total lie, seeing as when he escaped, he did plan to look.

"Thought so, you must be Jake. He talks about you a lot, and someone named Star?"

"His daughter. You've seen him?" Jake demanded.

"Yeah. Actually, I'm usually his guard. Except we have a shortage of scouts right now. After this trip, I'll be back on my regular rotation." He didn't elaborate why they were running low. "You should get some sleep. With Casper around, you probably won't get much." He deftly slipped a tranquilizer dart into his gun.

"Sorry about this," Dare apologized and shot the dart at Jake. His consciousness slipping away yet again, Jake felt his hands being untied, then retied in front of him. *At least this guy has some decency*, he thought and blacked out.

❂ ❂ ❂

"Dare!" Someone was calling his name. Whoever it was, they were really angry. "Dare! Get up!" Something slapped him. His eyes snapped open, just in time to see Casper drawing back his hand again.

"I'm awake! I'm awake!" He protested, lifting his arms to shield his face. Sitting up, he received another slap.

"You fell asleep on watch! The prisoner could have escaped!"

"No, he couldn't, I hit him with a dart, he's gonna be out cold for a couple more hours!" He sulked.

"That's just perfect! We have to get moving, and you're going to carry him!" Casper commanded angrily. "Good going moron!"

Dare groaned, *this is gonna be a long trip.*

❂ ❂ ❂

Jade was at a meeting. She, like any normal person, hated meetings. This particular meeting was a monthly update for all of the higher officers. Mainly all of the very top guys were there, with the exception of a few select scouts as eyewitnesses. These select three had actually managed to escape the terrors that threatened all of the recent scouts, or rather, the sadly departed scouts.

This is stupid! She thought. They'd had no choice recently, but to send out regular guards and army men. It was fine except for the fact that they'd had absolutely no training in that area, and were dying left and right. Of all the actual veterans, there were now only 14 still alive. No way were they going to send them all out on a couple of patrols; hence the regulars.

Now with stories circulating about some monsters attacking the patrols, no one was volunteering, especially with the dangerously high death rate. Jade sighed; it was getting harder to give orders. She supported the Darkist's ideas, but not their way of doing things, especially the policy on traitors. Oh yeah, that was strict, and worse, almost everyone was very paranoid and suspicious. Not the best combination, if you're having second thoughts.

She was probably in the worst position, being third in command of the whole thing. Not high enough to make a big impact on how things were done, but high enough so that if she did something wrong she would fall a long way down, ultimately to the grave. With this happy thought, her attention was brought back to the issue on hand.

"Commander Ruin, I'm leaving this issue with you." Her superior ordered. "See to it that it's taken care of, dismissed!"

The officers in attendance quickly got up and left, avoiding the stare of the highest man in power, the current almost-ruler of the ZΣЯΘs. Gathering her stuff together, Jade vaguely hoped she wouldn't be ordered to stay. Turning to go, she sighed as the General not only ordered her to stay, but to sit back down as well. "Ruin, do you have any idea what's up with the scout issue?"

"No sir, the general assumption is that the R&R are finally taking action against us." She gripped the edge of her seat. Darkist leader Erak Darke. She didn't like him very much; they had a strained relationship, over the fact that she had turned him down several times. Apparently he found her close enough to perfect. She, on the other hand, had no interest for him. "Personally, I think it's an outside force. According to Miss DragonSong, they're still disorganized."

"That may be Jade, but I wouldn't trust her. She is a double agent after all, and no one really knows who a double agent is working for except for the agent themselves."

"Understood, Sir. Permission to return to normal duties?"

"Permission granted." Erak looked like he was going to say more, but wisely shut his mouth. Jade smirked; *he'd better keep his mouth shut,* she thought. *No way am I going to tolerate Erak asking me out again, supreme leader or not!* The door clicked shut behind her, a feeling of smugness added to her usual cold demeanor.

✪   ✪   ✪

Jake groaned, everything hurt, and he could barely move. Slowly opening his eyes, the brunette found himself lying on a cot in a corner of a huge room, with light streaming through a glass domed ceiling. Something was shimmering outside the glass, slight waves running across its surface giving it away as a shield; small scale obviously, not a Forcefield, which was big enough to encircle a whole planet.

His eyes scanning the room, Jake saw a lot of tables and computer boards scattered around, as well as a bunch of pieces of... well he wasn't quite sure what they were. It almost looked like his brother's workshop, minus the fact that it was so huge. Seeing no one, he tried to sit up, grunting in pain. The last thing he remembered was that guard, knocking him out.

On a small table next to him were a note and a glass of some orange liquid. He read the note.

Be back soon. If you wake up and I'm not here drink the orange stuff, it'll help with the bruising. -R

Startled, he stared at the note; the handwriting was so familiar it could have been his own. *What was his name... Dare?* Jake thought. *He said something about being Robby's guard.* It all made sense now; this was where his brother was being held prisoner. He had to admit though, it was no dungeon; everything here was state of the art, shiny and brand new, except for the odd care-worn tool here and there.

Guessing it couldn't hurt his current situation, and too thirsty to care, he practically inhaled the strange liquid. It was ice cold, and sent a pleasant shock though his body. Almost immediately his headache began to fade, as well as his various injuries. Standing up, Jake wandered over to the nearest table and picked up a few pieces of paper, depicting very complicated blueprints. He hastily put them down not wanting to bring his headache back.

Strangely, he felt a little homesick, looking at the familiar mess of half-finished inventions. Wandering over to what appeared to be a snack bar of all things; he rummaged around and found an abundance of food. *Well, at least they aren't starving him,* Jake thought. All in all, he was confused with the situation. The only reason Robby would still be alive was that the Darkist wanted him, probably to make weapons or something.

He sighed, exploring his cell. Strangely enough, there didn't appear to be any visible kind of surveillance, but then again you never could tell with technology these days. Even the people of Earth had tiny cameras that would go unnoticed even to the experienced eye.

Whatever the case, the room would have been perfect, except for the fact that it was still a cell, however extravagant. Settling down on the couch at a small entertainment center, he flicked through various channels on the 3D wall screen. Not finding anything of interest, he decided to look at the digital files containing his brother's previous accomplishments, setting it to play all.

As the software presented different inventions and broke them down into components, describing what they did and how they worked; Jake zoned out, nodding off every now and then. The products themselves were interesting, and plainly useful, he didn't really care how they worked, so long as they did.

So, when someone entered the room from a teleportation pad- there were no doors- and came to stand behind Jake, he didn't notice. After a few seconds, the stranger coughed, causing Jake to whip around. He found himself staring into the face of Robert Gilgalad, who was grinning like crazy and trying to hold back his laughter.

"Hi!" he managed before giving in. "You should see the look on your face! Priceless!"

Jake resorted to brute force. Jumping over the couch, he tackled his brother to the ground. They were pretty evenly matched, considering that Robert was three years older and at least ten times stronger. But Jake had been working out.

"You little!" he exclaimed, laughing in spite of himself. After they had calmed down enough not to resemble two squealing children, Jake got down to business. "Okay, spill." He gave his brother a once over and noticed he looked a little more careworn, but surprisingly well kept, not a scratch on him.

A small beeping noise filled the air for a second and Robert frowned, wincing as if in pain. "What's wrong?" Jake asked concerned.

"Nothing important, but you're going to have to wait for an explanation." Robert replied, gathering up some things off one of the tables. He headed to the circle that marked the telepad. "You can come if you want; I just have to go present what I'm working on for inspection. It should only take about fifteen minutes."

He stepped onto the telepad, and Jake noticed a small earpiece connected to a flesh colored wire that trailed down to a flat square secured on the back of his brother's neck. Before he could get a closer look, Robert disappeared to the responding telepad. Deciding to follow, Jake followed suit and stepped onto the pad, vanishing out of the room.

CHAPTER 6

*R*un. It was the first thought on Gil's mind. *Run, you shouldn't be here.* He dashed through the city and into an alleyway. He was standing with his back to a wall, cornered. He had to get out of there, but how? Glancing around, he scanned the faces of his pursuers. He had done nothing wrong, but not one of them was going to let him live.

Going over his options, he frowned. *Stupid orders! Do not engage! Come on! I can totally beat them!* He growled in frustration. *Okay, surrender and be killed. Don't surrender, and be killed. Get the heck outta there, and avoid being killed. Yeah, I'm going to have to go with number three.*

He waited, wasting a few precious seconds. He had to think of a destination. *Fiji? No. R&R? Not right after a mission failure. Okay, I need a clear space... Preferably with no one nearby.* He nodded, and quickly typed a random code into his watch, waiting for the command to register. *Stupid outdated tech,* he thought.

"What are you doing?" One of the thugs asked suspiciously.

Ignoring his captors, he tapped the device irritatedly and concentrated on his destination, then vanished without a trace.

✪ ✪ ✪

Lester and Katie were obviously having a good time. They were off in some corner or other doing who knows what, trying to avoid their fan club. *Probably a lot of stuttering and compliment giving, without really getting to the point,* thought Starlight. *They're both pretty young, seeing as Lester's only eighteen and Katie... well she's young.*

Starlight wasn't really concerned, after all how much trouble could a couple of kids get into? *Don't jinx it,* she thought turning back to her own problems.

At least Arya had made sure no one knew what the fuss was about. She had pulled them into one of the buildings adjacent to her little gazebo, glared at Starlight for what seemed like forever, and said, "What is with you! Are you trying to annoy the heck out of me?"

Needless to say, by the time she was through with "you little (insert useless insults here)", Starlight was amazed that Arya hadn't exploded yet. No one could mistake her for anything but an- she tried out the new word- Illusionator, she was so red. Not only her hair, but her eyes, skin, clothes, and even the air around her seemed red.

Ben was attempting to do damage control, but failing miserably. Eventually he just sat down next to Arya, and let her calm down, his shoulder getting soaked in the process. The lovely session ended with a lot of making out and couple stuff while Starlight slipped away thoroughly disgusted, and completely tired out. Not wanting to rejoin to party but having no idea what to do instead- as no one had said anything about where they were going to sleep- she slipped past the guards into the surrounding trees.

Starting in what she assumed was the direction to the waterfalls; she eventually stumbled onto a tiny clearing only about five feet across. Directly in front of her was a narrow slit in the rocky cliffs, with a soft blue light emanating from within. Not sure what she was doing or why, she turned around and started to go back, not wanting to disturb the glow. Strangely enough as she did so, she found that the forest had disappeared. In its place was another cliff. *Okay, that's weird...*

Turning back to the crack, she felt something nudge her shoulder, pushing her forwards. *Alright, alright! I'm going.* She squeezed between the rocks, and tripped into a small cave. Looking back, she instantly regretted her decision; the opening had vanished. She was trapped. *D'arvit! Wow, I'm smart.* She mentally slapped herself. *Fine! What's this all about?*

She scanned her prison and noticed that "the glow" was getting brighter by the second. Feeling energy buzz around her, the air turned dry and it was getting harder to breathe. Almost in front of her face a ball of light was forming, sending out electric shocks, and heating up what was left of the air.

Everything around Starlight felt as if it was on fire, including her. Realizing there wasn't any air left to breathe; she started to panic silently, as the world started turning black. Her last thought wasn't "I'm going to die!", but "THIS IS FREAKIN' AWESOME!!!" Just before she blacked out, she felt a pair of strong arms catch her as everything that ever was, exploded.

✪ ✪ ✪

The world shook under the impact, knocking people off their feet as they started shouting.

Katie looked up, "What was that?"

"I don't know," replied Lester.

"Arya, are you alright?" asked Ben.

"Yeah, what was that?"

"Is everyone okay?"

"What do you think caused it?"

"Ow! My ears hurt!"

"EVERYONE!" someone shouted above the noise. "CALM DOWN!" The crowd instantly settled. "Whatever it was, it's over. We'll send out an investigation in the morning. For now you should all go to bed in case there are repercussions. Don't worry, nothing was broken, no one was hurt, and nobody died. Good night."

As it turned out, he was completely wrong on that account.

CHAPTER 7

Gil was pissed. Of course it was just his luck that he'd ended up in trouble, again. Luckily it hadn't been *his* trouble, but it was still trouble. Growling in frustration he punched the wall, his fist leaving a good sized dent. The roof shook, bits of the ceiling fell down. *Oops*, he thought. *That probably wasn't a good idea.*

He was sitting on the floor of a cave, next to a glowing cocoon of blue light. The girl inside was dead, that much he knew, but there was a chance that she'd be alright. She suddenly jerked to one side, narrowly missing a wall. *Well, if she doesn't bring down the roof in the process,* he amended.

He sighed, his anger gone. He was relieved that he had come when he did. That girl would have been blown to pieces. At least the cave held. In actuality, Gil was pretty much holding it together with his will and the remnants of energy from the explosion. It was a hard task, considering that he also has to periodically blast sparks at her.

Kind of a weird thing to do, blasting sparks at someone, he reflected. But it was essential for her survival. The excess amount of energy left over had fused together, creating a substance that most people called magic, and he called alien science. It had immediately targeted the girl, pouring itself into her DNA, changing her very existence. Magic was very volatile unless stored in something living or had a large amount of energy to begin with.

As a result, her body was undergoing a dramatic change, using more energy than it had stored. There was absolutely no way that she would survive on her own at this rate. *It's a good thing I'm here,* Gil laughed, unaware that the girl was fighting a losing battle.

He thought back on how he'd come to find himself in this position. It hadn't been his idea initially but his superior, if you could even call the man that. The R&R was in complete disarray and it was only getting worse. People were going missing, and he'd been given the task of finding them. The last mission had been a trap but he knew the R&R would deny it. There was probably several Darkist spies among their ranks; that or they just had the worst leaders in the history of ever.

But he had to say- they had some pretty decent tech.

He glanced down at the girl in front of him, wondering who she was and what she was doing in this random tiny dimension.

✪ ✪ ✪

Everything was black, but she could see perfectly, flashes of light lit the back of her mind. She was flying through an endless tunnel, falling down a bottomless pit. It was eerily quiet except for a faint crackling noise like a tiny fire on the edge of hearing. Sparks drifted past going in the opposite direction.

Go back, something was telling her. *Follow the sparks. Give in to the energy. Stay safe, go back.*

No, embrace the black. Close your eyes; push your limits. The two wills were pulling her in different directions. Relentlessly they bombarded her senses, fighting for control.

The smells of home, flashes of familiar faces, and the touch of a loving embrace battled against a sense of wonder, the thrill of adventure, and the taste of new things.

Come back. Live your life, stay with your friends.

Come explore the universe. Find its darkest secrets.

Go with the flow.

Adventure is calling.

COME BACK.

GO ON!

"STOP!" She couldn't take it anymore; they were pushing her beyond her limits, she was past the breaking point.

DECIDE!

NOW!

"NO!" She lashed out, disturbing the flow of the sparks. They swirled around her, lifting her up, forming a shield around her. Something clicked in her mind, and the sparks entered her, blending with her very essence, bringing new memories, knowledge, and power she didn't want.

Standing her ground, she called the sparks together, rising through the black towards a light above her. Breaking free of the depths, she was drawn back to reality. Feeling the hard ground beneath her was a relief. She opened her eyes and looked around confused. She was standing at the bottom of a grassy hill facing a flight of dirt stairs. The sky was completely dark, not a single star to be seen. She frowned slowly turning in a circle seeing nothing but the hill. It was as if nothing but the hill existed.

This is weird, she thought. *Where am I?*

She started to climb the stairs. She could just make out a faint glow coming from the top. As she got closer, the glow got a lot stronger until she was almost blinded, but yet she could see just fine. Once at the top, a new world came into view. The stairs turned into a wide dirt path and the bright glow was coming from dead ahead. She could see a range of mountains ahead and to the right with a red glow emanating from the bottom but it was dim in comparison. To her left was a wall of mist, so thick she couldn't even see an inch through it.

Starlight squinted trying to see what was making the light, but it was too far away. So she started walking and after what seemed like years, she finally came to a crossroads. The bright white glow was coming from a shining white city ahead. Her feet were drawn to it but she firmly planted them and looked to her right. There was a path with bits of twisted metal winding down the slope to a hole in the bottom of the nearest mountain. Even from that distance she could feel the heat rolling off in waves.

Turning to the left, she saw that a path led into the mist. It was somehow more alluring to her than the city, but she refrained from walking into the unknown. *At least for now*, she thought. Deciding to take a chance on the city, she started walking. The closer she got, the more details she noticed. Everything was bright and colorful and the sky over the city wasn't black but an indistinguishable color, like a mix of every color ever made and some she knew were there but couldn't even see.

At the gate there was two shining figures, one holding a glowing sword, and the other holding a glowing book. *Okay, what's with all the glowing things?* she thought to herself. She stood awkwardly looking between the two angels- *What else could they be?*

"Hi. Where am I?" Starlight felt the urge to hold her hands behind her back like she was a little kid.

"The Gates of Heaven child. Do you wish to enter?" Asked the one with the book.

"Uh... I don't know, am I dead?"

"No."

"Oh. Um... sure? Can I get some answers if I go in?" she tilted her head to the side.

"That depends on what you wish answered."

"Right. Okay then. I guess I'll go in?" Sword Angel turned and the gates opened allowing them to go inside. She followed the angel through the city and up to a building in the center that seemed to be the light source. She was then handed off to a different angel and taken inside. Passing an open set of doors with light streaming through she caught a glimpse of the brightest light yet, but they went by too quickly. Turning into a side room, Starlight was left alone with the promise that someone would be there shortly.

She sat down on the sofa, one of the only articles of furniture besides the white marble coffee table and an identical sofa on the other side. There was a window overlooking the city opposite the door where she could see people going about their business. *Everything was so bright,* she frowned. There was a knock at the door.

"May I come in?" The voice was vaguely familiar, like someone she used to know but hadn't seen them in forever.

"Yes," she called, eyes trained to the door. For some unfathomable reason she was nervous. A woman entered, followed by a man. They were both dressed in similar looking white robes with smooth blue cords around their waists and gold circlets on their heads.

"Hello Star." The woman said.

"Hello..." she glanced between the two. The man had light brown hair and bright blue eyes while his skin was a dark tan. The woman was significantly paler than he and had brown eyes and auburn hair. Again, they seemed oddly familiar.

"Don't you remember us?" the man asked smiling.

"No- Yes- I don't know... I feel like I should." Starlight said.

"What *do* you remember?"

"Uh, my name..." she hesitated. "That's it really. But there are other things, things that aren't my memories."

"Aren't they?" the woman laughed.

CHAPTER 8

Dare was back on rotation, and relieved to get out of any more patrols. He'd heard the rumors, but hadn't seen anything strange, besides the odd spark here and there. The sparks were unique to Planet Four. No one knew exactly what caused them, but they were probably left over from all the energy flying around after the shutdown of the portals. Four had been a center of trade and communication in the ΖΣЯΘs, people going through from almost every sector, dimension, and Universe in existence.

Now, they were closed and off the radar. It was a pity that the Darkist had decided to stop the activity, information was much easier to get when people started gossiping. Standing at his usual post outside the opposite end of the inventor's telepad, he glanced at the monitors. Jake had just reunited with his brother and there was a lot of pushing and shoving. When they came through the pad, he nodded.

"Robert, you're back."

"Yup, they want to see the latest update."

Dare shook his head, "You've been busy today haven't you?"

"Yeah well, you know, people to do, stuff to see."

Jake laughed, "You're still saying that?"

"Yup, come Oh brother o' mine." Robert led his brother down the elegant wood lined hallway and through a system of twists and turns.

"How do you remember where you're going?"

"I've been doing it for so long; I don't even have to look where I'm going."

"Yeah, so how come they just let you walk around here? There's like no guards."

"I'll explain later. Here we are." Robert pushed the door open entered, motioning for Jake to wait.

He reappeared and pulled Jake into the room. There was a huge table with empty chairs lined up along the sides. Standing at the head of the table was a woman, with long brown hair tied in a ponytail and an impatient frown on her face. "Robert, hurry up and get this over with, I have problems I need to get to."

"Right, sorry Jade. Okay this here is the finished model of the..." Jake tuned him out focusing on the woman. *She looks familiar,* he thought frowning. *A light went off in his head. That guard, Dare. That's who she looks like. I wonder if they're related?*

He glanced at a clock on the table. 3 o'clock in the afternoon. The room looked like a conference room, complete with coffee machine. *At least I hope that's a coffee machine,* he thought. The view from the windows looked out onto the city. Kapital City, home of the greatest technological marvels in the ΖΣЯΘs. Jake sighed, *too bad that it's closed off. And taken over by the Darkist.*

Robert had finished his presentation and Jade focused on him. "Your brother, I presume?"

"Yes," Robert replied. "This is Jake."

"Hi." Jake was getting nervous under the woman's intense stare. Her brown eyes held a sort of deep pain masked by an obsidian shell.

"Yes, you two look alike."

"So we've been told." Jake replied. He cleared his throat, "May I ask a second question?"

Jade blinked, confused at his random remark. "What?"

"Well," Jake explained. "I just asked a question when I was asking if I could ask a second one. So may I ask a third?"

"You only asked- What is your question?" Jade glared.

"I was just wondering if you were related to Dare?"

"Why didn't- never mind. Yes, he's my brother. Robert-" Robert's attention snapped back to woman. "You better take your brother back to your room. Your projects are all on schedule so there is no reason for you to still be here."

"Uh- right sorry. Come on Jake." Robert nodded towards the door. With a last glance at Jade, Jake followed, happy to get away from that menacing woman's stare.

Catching up with his brother, he whispered "So how are you? They treat you okay?"

"Yeah, I'll explain when we get back to my room. So how have you been? Is Star okay?"

"She's fine, I think. I don't actually know where she is at the moment, seeing as we got separated getting here."

"How *did* you get here?"

"Well, the portal in our basement randomly started working and stucked us up, then we landed in this crazy girl's hideout, then Star's..." Jake hesitated. "Necklace, took me and Kegan here and I don't know where Starlight and Katie went."

"I'm guessing Katie is the crazy girl, but who's Kegan?"

"The stupid Portalshroom that followed us. Where is he for that matter, not that I'm complaining- he just won't shut up!"

"I'll ask. He's probably locked up somewhere if he's that annoying." They had turned onto the right hallway and Robert nodded at Dare. The brothers stepped onto the telepad and entered Robert's room.

"I'm not sure how much I can tell you," Robert started off after they had taken a seat. "But I'll do my best."

Jake leaned in, awaiting his brother's recap of the years they had spent apart.

"How much do you know about Starlight?"

✪ ✪ ✪

Starlight looked at the woman frowning slightly. "But they can't be my memories, I've never done any of that... Have I?" She thought back through the confusing mess. She saw flashes of the two in front of her but they were jumbled in with things from different times. Everything was out of order.

"Star," the man said sharply.

"Yes Father?" She blinked. "Wait what?" He was grinning. The women- no her *mother*- was laughing.

"Hello Star."

"Mother?" Starlight shook her head as the memories kept swirling around inside her brain. "How? What?"

"Who, where, when, why?" a younger voice laughed cutting through her confusion. "Hey Star! Long time no see!" She looked up and standing at the door was a blonde haired, blue eyed young man.

"Bunny?" She stared incredulously.

He bowed. "The one and only! Come give your brother a hug!"

"Bunny? But-"

The young man smothered her in a big hug, putting an end to her protests. "Hey, it's okay! Just relax Star. Let's sit down, shall we?"

The family complied and Starlight found herself sitting next to her brother on the sofa. She looked each of them over, as if trying to memorize them and said, "Okay. Explain. 'Cause I'm confused. And I really don't like being confused."

Bunny- she really *did* have to remember his real name- laughed. "I've got this one. Okay so you remember the Move?"

She opened her mouth, "...No..."

"Okay what *do* you remember?"

"From the beginning?"

"Yeah."

She sighed, "It's all mixed up. You're telling me they're memories, but I don't remember that stuff ever happening. I *do* remember growing up with Jake in a house on Earth, and trying to fix that stupid Portal practically every day. Then all this crazy stuff after said Portal randomly started working."

She sat back and crossed her arms.

"Okay. Well, that's a start." Bunny said. "A small- no tiny- start." He grinned, "But that's better than nothing. You have the other memories at least. That's good. So let me tell you a story..."

✪ ✪ ✪

Robert sighed. *Where to start?* "Jake, you remember that government agent coming to our house about a month before Star was born?"

"Yeah, what was up with that?"

"Well, they came about Star."

"But she wasn't born yet." Jake frowned confused.

"Wrong. She was dying."

Jake looked at his brother like he had just told him that he was a girl.

"No, listen. I'm sure you've noticed how Star can change how she looks."

"Yeah, her hair changes color when she loses control of her emotions. So? That's normal for kids here. Infused energy from the Move, you know that."

"Yes, but let's have a short history lesson." Robert's voice was patiently sarcastic. "Most people know the story of Atlantis, technologically advanced city lost to the sea. But technically that's only partly true. Atlantis was built right on top of the largest Portal Crystal cache ever, nine crystals. The founders of Atlantis discovered them and soon after discovered the ΖΣЯӨs. Atlantis became a center of trade and dimensional travel and is home to the Hall of Portals. Unfortunately, the city wasn't equipped for the amount of energy it possessed and kept letting off ribbons of energy that eventually made their way to the Darkist. The Darkist attempted to attack the city to take hold of the Portal Crystals but in a desperate attempt to save their city, the Atlanteans moved the city to an unoccupied planet in the Isis dimension, called Planet Four because of its location in relation to its star."

"I know that." Jake said sarcastically.

Robert glanced around the room then pointedly looked at his brother. *We're being watched.*

Jake nodded, closing his eyes as if tired. Robert continued, "Second history lesson. You remember the royal Atlantean family right before the Move?"

"Yes, the queen died on the way here and the princess went missing. But the King and prince survived and set up the new planet and Kapital City. There's statues of them everywhere."

"You remember how the princess was born?"

"Yes. The queen had come into contact with raw Portal Crystal energy, but instead of dying, the energy transferred to her unborn child, turning the girl into a Blender, able to change her DNA at will. She was born with dark skin, white hair and bright purple eyes, not looking like anyone from her family but taking on the rarest qualities of their people and combining them into one appearance."

"Long explanation but, yes that's how it happened. So this new princess was named Star- I don't know why- and was loved by her people. The day of the Move, she mysteriously disappeared, most likely killed in the resulting chaos."

"But she wasn't!" Jake exclaimed, comprehension dawning on his face.

"No she wasn't. It's impossible for Blenders to die, their bodies naturally taking on immortal qualities. So what is she supposed to do after a normal lifespan ends and all the people she knows are dead?"

Jake was silent.

"She and the Four government came to the agreement that she would be adopted after every time she 'died'. She would repress her memories, waiting for a trigger- usually something the foster family and her agreed upon- until she was sixteen. This time around it was my turn. The government contacted me and Rose- her foster mother- and set up a date to transfer her."

"The day she was born," Jake nodded. "Which just so happened to be the day the Darkist came in."

"Yup. I can tell you this because they already know about her."

"They were looking- *are* looking for her." Jake stated.

"Yes. So it's a good thing you don't know where she is. I'm currently working on a device that can access someone's memories without harm. It's almost done which is good and bad. Good, because that means torture will be pointless so there's no reason for it. But bad, because they can get any information they want, and there's no resistance. But at least they'll have the truth, for court cases and stuff." Robert shrugged lamely.

"*This* is the kind of stuff they've been having you make?" Jake asked incredulously.

"They have enough weapons, so why would they want more? They want information. Have you been questioned yet?"

"No. I just woke up here after getting captured."

"Then watch what you say, there's cameras in here obviously, but I'm being watched too. You asked why I can just walk around wherever I want?" he sighed, shaking his head. "I'm loaded with trackers and stuff. Even if I did manage to escape, they'd know exactly where to find me." He shrugged and stared at the wall.

Jake wasn't sure what to say. It was a lot to take in. His Starlight, an Atlantean princess, billions of years old. And a Blender to boot. As for Robert, he'd expected no less from the Darkist but some things just didn't quite add up.

Robert had his thinking expression on his face and was staring intently at the wall. As Jake watched him, he suddenly stiffened and winced. A loud beeping sound was heard and Robert shut his eyes tightly, his hands holding his head as he bent forward. It stopped after a few seconds, leaving him annoyed and rubbing his head. As his brother bent over, Jake saw the square on the back of his neck light up, and attributed the noise to the earpiece.

Robert took a breath and said calmly, "Thinking of upcoming projects, and Star."

A male voice coming from a speaker somewhere in the room responded, "You know the rules Gilgalad."

The inventor nodded and turned to Jake, who was staring at him. "What was that?" Jake demanded. "One of those security measures you talked about?"

"Yes. It measures my brainwaves and if they go above a certain level, well…" he shrugged. "I'd rather not talk about it."

Jake frowned, but respected his brother's request. "So that invention you're making... It's for you isn't it?"

Robert smiled, "Yeah, I give them a pretty good workout with this method. They don't know what I'm thinking, only that I am."

"So put escaping with you out of my head?"

"Definitely."

CHAPTER 9

"Enter Atlantis," Bunny said dramatically. "Best place in the ZΣЯΘs! Or it was, until the Darkist came in. Now- me, Mother, Father, and *you* were the rulers of Atlantis at the time. Fifth generation or something- not important. But! Our fair city was located on the biggest cache of Portal Crystals ever, so far as anyone knows. The Darkist- led by Erak Darke, the crazy OCD emperor- want to make the ZΣЯΘs perfect. Impossible goal but that's *their* problem. They believe that Portal Crystals can help them do that- you do remember what Portal Crystals are right?"

Starlight nodded, rolling her eyes.

"Good. So as I was saying. They wanted Portal Crystals to 'fix' everything, so they decided to steal the biggest batch they could find. Go figure. But we were warned of their attack and set about relocating the city. Picked a random planet, in a random dimension and started the Move."

"But something went wrong."

"Yeah. Unfortunately. The amount of energy from the Crystals was unstable and about a fourth of the Population died."

"Including Mother." Starlight said.

"Yeah. But that's all good now. Anyway, you got lost. Ended up... somewhere, and the Darkist found you. The story round here is that you majorly pissed off Erak and

53

since then he's been looking for you. You found your way back to the new location, now named Planet Four, and set up a deal with the government-"

"That I would be passed from family to family after a normal lifespan. I'm starting to remember this bit." She interrupted.

"Perfect and around the time you'd turn sixteen you'd get your memories back- you're sixteen now aren't you?"

Starlight nodded. "So how long does it take to get all my memories organized?"

Bunny hesitated, looking at their parents. "You guys wanna take this bit?"

Her mother smiled, "Well, you never really do. You've been traveling all over the ZΣЯΘs and have more memories than you're supposed to. You simply don't have room for them all. That's another reason that you made that deal, so you don't have to deal with constant headaches."

"Uh huh. So I need something to store them all in?"

"That would probably be a good idea. But you have to go soon." Her mother smiled.

"Star?" her father asked.

"Yes?"

"Be careful. I don't want to see you permanently stuck here for a long time." He grinned.

"I'll try, but no promises. So where do I go now?"

"Well, I would assume you'd go back to where you came here from."

"Could I go somewhere else?" she frowned. "I don't really want to go back to that tiny cave."

"Your body is still there." her mother said. "So unless you could move it…"

"Right. Cave it is then. I'll see you again?" She asked, looking around at her long lost family.

"Yes, probably sooner than you think." Bunny grinned.

"Bunny?"

"Yes."

"What's your real name? I can't remember."

"Lewis."

"Oh."

He grinned, "Well, see ya."

She laughed and hugged each of them before making her way to the door. Another angel waited outside to escort her to the gates. The journey out was slower than the one in, allowing her to fully appreciate the splendor of the city. Children laughed and chased each other around, while adults mingled. Most were smiling, and those that weren't, were laughing. It was very infectious and she soon found a grin breaking across her face.

They reached the gates and the angel bid her farewell. "Yeah, see ya," Starlight nodded. The gates opened and she walked out.

"I trust you found the answers you sought?" asked Book Angel.

"Enough to pretend to know what I'm doing." she laughed.

"Good then. I trust you know your way."

"Yeah… just follow the road back down the stairs…"

"And walk into the Void."

"Right, thanks. There's no hurry, right?" She asked.

His eyes twinkled and he looked straight ahead. Starlight nodded, turned, and started walking. She soon reached the Crossroads and turned to look back at the shining city. The mist was still there on her left, and she felt sure the angel had meant she could take a few moments to explore. *After all, there's no Time here, right?*

She walked over to the left road and stuck her hand into the Mist. It parted slightly and swirled around her fingers. She grinned and walked into the mist vanishing from sight.

✪ ✪ ✪

Jake was lounging on the couch listening to Robert working on the newest project, throwing a ball into the air and catching it. "So are they going to question me?"

"I don't know." Robert grabbed something off the table and started loosening something. Jake idly watched his progress, catching the ball again.

"So what are we going to do?"

"Hope Star has remembered everything and knows what to do."

"No escape attempts, hope of rescue, sabotage?"

"Nope." Robert popped the p. "But you're welcome to try. You won't get anywhere, and they probably won't let you stay in here anymore."

"Good point. So Star it is?"

"Yup."

"Robby?"

"Yeah?"

"Any idea why our Portal started working that day?" Jake leaned over to catch the ball.

"Well," Robert grunted, straining to tighten whatever it was. "The Darkist have been jamming all the Portals, so unless they stopped or someone managed to hack yours, I have no idea."

"So you could just call it destiny then?"

"More like really bad luck." They lapsed into a comfortable silence.

"Robby? I'm bored."

"Then watch TV."

"You have TV?"

"Just Darkist propaganda channels and misinformed news stations, but yeah. You could try getting Dare to take you on a tour or to the store or something."

"I can leave the compound?"

"What's stopping you?"

"Good question. Uhh, I'll be back sooner or later then." Jake said, moving towards the door.

Robert waived in recognition, never taking his eyes off his work. Jake stepped onto the telepad and left the room. Glancing around, he saw Dare lounging on a chair playing some kind of videogame. The guard looked up and smiled, "Hey Jake, what can I do for you?"

"Robert says that you could give me a tour or take me somewhere outside?"

"Uh... let me check with my superiors." he touched a button on his thick black bracelet and said, "Uh, yeah this is Ruin, Gilgalad's brother wants to know if he can go outside or something... Yeah... No, I'll keep an eye on him... Okay, sure. That works."

Jake watched as Dare turned to him and said, "You've got clearance, but we have to wait until a replacement gets here in a few minutes."

"That's fine." Jake grinned. "So, Kapital City changed any in the last sixteen years?"

"You'd be surprised." Dare nodded grimly. "All the buildings are intact, but there's a lot of propaganda and the citizens mostly stay inside. The streets are perfectly safe, but I guess no one really likes risking anything. Oh, hey James." He addressed the last line to another guard. "Well, I guess we'll be going then. Thanks mate."

James nodded and sat down on the chair. "Mind if I continue the game?"

"Go ahead, so long as you get me up in levels." Dare grinned.

James nodded and was soon absorbed in the game. Dare and Jake made their way out of the compound and Jake took in the spectacle of his home city. The buildings were still white, none of the architecture was damaged, or had been repaired, and the streets were clean. There were a few citizens outside, but Dare had been right, most were inside. They walked over to Kapital Mall and went inside.

"Never thought I'd walk in here with a Darkist agent." Jake shook his head, smiling.

"What about a friend?"

"You're my friend?"

"I'm friends with most everyone. Was in the Four military before the Darkist came."

"I see."

"It was 'join or die'; don't judge."

"I'm not judging. So where to?"

"Ice cream? I don't usually get to have recreational time when I'm on duty."

"Yeah, about that- how come security is so..."

"Relaxed? They've got the Forcefield up, no one can get in or out, so why have everything be hush hush? They're so confident and have enough security. They don't mess much with Four government or its people. Just drafted the military and use Four as they're 'home away from home' as it were. Life goes on as normal here."

"But Four is a center of trade! What about the Hall of Portals?" Jake asked.

Dare shrugged. "Darkist are blocking the Portals, only Darkist approved stuff gets through- throughout the ZΣЯΘs."

"Wow. I didn't know their influence was that massive yet."

"Well, you *have* been out of the loop for about sixteen years." Dare grinned. "So how was Earth working for you?"

"A lot like here really, just without the perks of our technology."

"Well, we *did* technically originate from Earth. Or rather, a version of Earth." Dare laughed. "So what flavor? Something exotic, or boring and overused."

"Mint?"

"Boring and overused it is then. I'll have vanilla and he'll have mint." his guard told the man behind the counter.

"Oh, so vanilla isn't 'boring and overused'?"

"Not when I'm ordering it?" Dare grinned. "Thank you. Here." He handed Jake the cones while he paid the man.

"Come again," the man said laughing at their banter.

"Where to next?" Dare asked. "We've got about two hours."

"I'm no teenage girl, but I *do* need some clothes. Are you paying?"

"Sure thing, off we go!"

By the time they were done, Jake had learned that the Dare's older sister was in charge of the entire Four division, the R&R really *was* terrible at their job, and that if Starlight was caught by the Darkist- there was the *tiny* problem of their impending doom.

He also found out first hand why people called his guard 'Dare'. "I think you missed a display," he remarked sarcastically.

Dare just laughed, and helped the employees to clean up the carnage he had left in his wake. Jake was NEVER challenging the guard to doing gymnastics in a dress again.

✪ ✪ ✪

The desk was a mess. *This just won't do. No, not at all.* Erak frowned, and started rearranging everything. Half an hour later he sat back and sighed rubbing his teal eyes. *There, that's better.* He glanced at the clock. *Just in time for the meeting. Perfect. And if anyone is late...* he let the thought trail off with a scowl. Someone knocked on the door. "Enter." Erak said, rearranging his features.

The door opened and Joshua, his upstart second in command, stuck his head in. "The meeting is in five minutes, Sir. Are you ready?"

"Yes, let's go. Is Jade going to be there?" He smiled.

"Yes Sir, all the division heads will be there."

"Good. I've had a new idea."

"Sir?" Joshua turned to look at him, his light purple eyes staring at Erak.

"First tell me if there's been any progress on finding the R&R."

"No sir. Although we've recently found one of their agent's hideouts. I'm sure you're aware of the name Katie Boardo."

"That's their head tech, correct?"

"Yes. We received a signal from one of the Portals. The Earth-7 portal randomly started transmitting." Joshua frowned. "Normally this wouldn't be a problem, but someone managed to turn on a receiving Portal. Two beings, identified as-" he checked his clipboard, "a Jake and Starlight Gilgalad, ended up on an Unclassified moon somewhere in the Fio dimension."

"Boardo's hideout."

"Exactly. We sent a team in, but there was no one there. Although..." Joshua hesitated. "We did find evidence of a Portal Crystal cache. It was removed before we got there, however and there was no trace of a Portalshroom."

"Didn't we apprehend a Jake Gilgalad and a Portalshroom on Four?" Erak frowned, thinking.

"Yes. But Boardo and Starlight are still missing."

"And the hideout?"

"Annexed as Darkist property, and left well guarded in case of their return."

"Good, send out a warrant for their arrest. I don't care what you do with Boardo, but I want this Starlight alive."

"Do you think she's..."

"Yes. I'm certain she is."

CHAPTER 10

Starlight sat up and opened her eyes, seeing a boy staring at her in surprise.

"Who are you?" he asked, tentatively as if a loud noise would shatter her.

She stared at the boy. He had bright green hair, burnt orangey-yellow eyes, and tan skin. Her head was spinning and she had the biggest headache of her life.

"I'm Starlight. Who are you?" she asked. *Starlight.* That name held so many new meanings. She had memories that were her own, but weren't. *Starlight.* An infinity of memories from different times. She shook her head, trying to process everything.

"My name's Gil. Are you alright? That was a pretty big explosion." He blinked at her a bit confused. "I must admit, I've never seen anything like that, and I've seen a lot."

Explosion. That's right, she had been in an explosion. "What exploded?" she asked.

"Um... *You*, I think. What happened just before?"

"I got sick of a party so I went exploring. I found this little clearing thing and a crack in the cliff that was glowing. I didn't want to mess with it, so I started to go back, but the clearing had disappeared. I felt something pushing me so I went inside but the opening had disappeared too. Then everything got bright and exploded."

"Has it ever happened before? The explosion thing?"

"No, I've- yes actually, now that I think about it." She'd usually regain her memories a bit explosively. "Okay, I don't know what's going on. I was fine before the explosion, but now my head hurts- which isn't weird- but I've got all these other memories that aren't mine, but they are and I don't know where they came from but I'm starting to remember and-" Starlight realized that she was hyperventilating.

"Woah, slow down!" Gil laughed. "Your hair is changing colors."

"Oh, yeah. It does that."

Gil gave her a funny look. "You can change your appearance to anything? And it's actually physical?"

"Yes..." she hesitated, thinking. Her memories were still confusing, but had started to lock into place, as if finding their correct spots and settling down. "I'm something called an-"

"Blender?"

Starlight stopped dead. She had heard that word before- in her other memories. "I was going to say Illusionator but that's not right. Blender, yes that's it. I'm a Blender." She frowned, "What's a Blender?"

Gil laughed at her. "This," he said, rapidly changing his appearance, "is a Blender." His hair settled back into its green color.

"But that's what an Illusionator does..."

"No, an Illusionator make *illusions*, hence the name. It's not actually physically there unless they're really powerful- and even then it's not *real*. No, a Blender can physically change their DNA at will into anything." He paused, then changed his voice to a narrator's dramatic deep tone. "They can match any person's DNA and can literally become anyone and anything. Therefore any 'super power' that is part of someone's DNA can be replicated using that specific set of DNA. Also, any defects in that person's DNA can be filtered out and superior genetics filtered in thus creating the ultimate being." he laughed. "So basically, a Blender can be anything they want and are kinda sorta unable to die, as far as I'm aware."

"Oh. Well that's..." *Inconvenient,* she thought.

"Yeah, so how old are you?"

Sixteen, she was about to say, but it ended up coming out as, "I don't know. Old, *really* old."

"Where are you from?"

"Planet Four," she blinked. "Yes, no- *Atlantis.*"

Gil looked at the girl in surprise. "Atlantis? The Planet Four Atlantis?"

"Yes." Starlight frowned. "I remember now... So *that's* who the Darkist are!"

"Didn't you know who they are?"

"No, not until now really. I was raised on Earth, 'cause Four was attacked by the Darkist the day I was born. We've got some history, their leader and I. He really doesn't like me. But that's normal, considering I try to annoy, sabotage his work, and generally make a nuisance of myself every time I get the chance."

"Makes sense." Gil nodded. "But how are you from Atlantis? That was *ages* ago. You sure you don't mean some copy of Atlantis?"

"Nope, I mean the real original Atlantis that's now currently on Planet Four. By the way, do you have any idea where the Darkist have their home base?"

"So far as I know, on your planet. But you still haven't answered my question."

"Princess Star of Atlantis at your service." she grinned, giving a mock bow.

"No way! You're not her!"

"Prove it." she shrugged. "I'm a Blender, I'm from Atlantis, and I'm still alive. Coinkydink? I don't think so."

"Then where have you been all this time, *Princess*?"

"Four's gov and I have come to a little agreement. I forget about my past until I'm a certain age, and get passed from foster family to foster family, each time living a normal lifespan." Starlight kicked at the dirt. Another piece of the ceiling fell. She looked around and suddenly noticed the concentrated look on Gil's face. "Are you holding this place up?"

"Yeah, so finish talking so we can get out of here, or rather, let's get out of here, then finish talking."

"Good idea. Where do we go? The entrance is gone."

"I don't think there ever was an entrance. This is some kind of in-between space. You most likely fell through a dimensional rift. But it's fine 'cause I've got a Transporter."

"So do I."

"Nice, well, where are we going?"

"Anywhere other than here."

"R&R headquarters it is."

"You work for the R&R?"

"Well…"

"Let me guess, just in it for the tech?"

"And the free food!"

"What is with everyone these days?" Starlight rolled her eyes. "Okay, meet you there?"

"You go first," Gil nodded.

"*Activation code.* R&R headquarters." she said clearly holding the necklace, and immediately vanished.

Gil was left alone. "*Travel.* R&R headquarters."

The cave collapsed.

As soon as Starlight said her destination she suddenly appeared in the middle of what looked like a crowded atrium. Everyone was staring at her. A few seconds later

Gil appeared. "Nothing to see here," he said, steering her towards one of the side doors.

They made their way through the hallways and up an elevator. Gil took a set of keys from his pocket and unlocked a door. He nudged her in and flipped on the lights. "Welcome to my office!" he said throwing himself into the chair behind the desk. "Close the door would you?"

Starlight complied, closing the door. "What were we talking about?"

"Uh, stuff."

"That's helpful."

"Planet Four, Darkist, you, stuff."

"That's better. Any questions?"

Gil looked around the room, thinking. "Nope. Not at the moment. No- wait. What do you plan on doing now?"

"Good question. I suppose I should tell my friends that I'm still alive and all that, then I'm going to look for my uncle."

"Adopted uncle according to you."

"Your point?" Silence. "I thought so."

"Any idea where he is?"

"Katie- my friend, suggested Four."

"Good place to start. So how did you end up in that cave?"

"Well..." She told him the whole story, ending with, "And then we came here. Where is 'here' by the way?"

"Some abandoned galaxy so remote that not even the Darkist know about it."

"Oh. So, message?"

"Right, you can use the Transporter, just say 'message', the location, and the person's name. It has to be a specific location though, like a city."

"Okay, I don't know Katie's last name... but I do know Lester's. Okay, like this. Wisdom's Valley, Lester Greylance?"

"You need the planet or galaxy and dimension."

"Dang, uh..."

"Your Transporter should have recorded the place when you went there. Here," he took her necklace and said, "Playback destinations."

"R&R headquarters, 16th galaxy, dimension unknown. Unclassified, dimension unknown. Wisdom's Valley, 82th galaxy, Kijn dimension. Unclassified, 13th galaxy, Fio dimension. Earth, 74th galaxy, Omega dimension. Planet Four, 39th galaxy, Isis dimension. End playback," said a smooth male computerized voice.

"Cool, it has a customized voice! Well there's your answer I guess. You haven't been many places."

"I have too! Just not with this thing!" she waved the necklace in his face.

"My mistake."

Rolling her eyes she touched the gem and said, "Message, Wisdom's Valley, 82th galaxy, Kijn dimension, Lester Greylance."

Nothing happened. "So, is this thing on?" she asked Gil.

He nodded saying, "You only get an image if the other person had a Transporter too. They can see and hear you, but you can only hear them. Inconvenient but better than nothing. They can't hear me."

"Okay, here goes nothing. Hey guys. I just wanted to say that I was caught in an explosion in some nowhere place. I'm fine though. It was just dimensional interference."

"There shouldn't be any problems on their end."

"Gil says that there shouldn't be any problems on your end. Oh yeah, I met Gil. He works for the R&R too. Katie, know him? Anyway, I'm going to head to Planet Four to find Jake. If you need to contact me just call the R&R. They'll get a message to me through Gil."

He nodded.

"Yeah, okay I think that's it. This is weird, I feel like I'm talking to no one. Okay bye." She looked at Gil. "How do I turn it off?"

"Say 'end call'."

"End call."

✪ ✪ ✪

Katie woke up the next morning confused. *That definitely isn't my ceiling*, she thought. Sitting up, she remembered the day before, vaguely wondering where Starlight had gotten off to. *Whatever, it isn't my problem.* She hopped out of bed and looked around. She had been having too much fun last night, and couldn't quite remember when or how she had gotten to her room. *Lester was totally flirting with me!* she giggled. She found a dress- *they tend to wear dresses here a lot-* and followed her nose to breakfast.

Lester was already there and had saved her a seat. "Hey."

"Hey," she blushed slightly. *He sure is cute!*

"Have you seen your friend anywhere? No one could find her last night."

"No, I'm sure she's around here somewhere though." Katie brushed the question off. "Any idea where that boom came from?"

"It was by one of the cliffs. However, there is no evidence of any damage. It's quite odd." Lester frowned.

"Yeah, I can run a scan of the area. See if there was any kind of interference."

"That would be a good idea. I'll try to find your friend."

"She's not my- oh never mind." Katie watched as Lester got up and spoke to one of the guards, walking out with him.

She sighed and finished eating her food, before getting up and making her way to the said cliffs. A few guards were standing around trying to find any signs of anything. Katie pulled out a small handheld device and began sweeping the area. She saw Lester and Arya walk over and shook her head. "There's a little energy left over from whatever it was, but there's no signs of any lasting effects. Whatever it was is long gone now."

"Good work." Lester smiled. "However, I couldn't find your friend. Do you know where she could have gone?"

"No, I only met her yesterday. And she's not my friend."

"Oh, my apologies. Perhaps-" Lester was cut off by a blue shape materializing out of nowhere. It solidified and took on the outlines of Starlight.

"Hey, is this thing on?..."

Once the message had finished Lester and Katie looked at each other. "Is that normal?" Lester asked.

"I don't know. I'm guessing she used her Transporter so I suppose so. If you're asking if that's normal for the R&R then no. So far as I know, only three members have one. Gil- Gillian, Viper, and Robert Gilgalad- Starlight's father. I don't really talk to the other members much though. Don't particularly like the R&R. Disorganized, terrible or no leaders, and can't agree on anything." Katie scoffed, grinning.

"Sounds awful." Lester said, his eyes twinkling. "And you still work for them?"

"Yeah I-" her demeanor changed and smile faded. "I didn't tell you I worked for them." She glared frostily at the prince.

He raised his hands in surrender. "I might know a little more about the R&R than I let on. Arya and myself are members but they haven't called us in so we didn't really feel the need to volunteer for anything."

"Are you? And why didn't you tell me this?"

"It never came up." He shrugged. "Arya?"

"What?"

"In the mood to visit our fellow members?"

"Why not? How do we get there?"

"Remember the Kiosk Incident...?"

"Oh no! We are *NOT* taking that infernal spaceship again!" Arya glared at him.

"You only didn't like it cause *I* was driving. Katie, can you drive a spaceship?"

Katie replied with a mischievous grin, "When do we start?"

CHAPTER 11

"Hey Gil, do you think it'd be a good idea if I sent a message to Jake?" The two were sitting in the mess hall eating lunch.

"I don't know, if he's on Four then the Darkist probably got a hold of him or he's hiding, and calling him might give him away. If there was a way to know what he was doing..." Gil trailed off.

"Can my Transporter do something like that?"

"Well, where'd you get it?"

"My- Robert made it. I don't know what settings it has or how it works really. Is there like a menu I could pull up?"

"Well... it would depend on the commands. Most people that make a Transporter make the commands universal, like playback destinations, message, and stuff. You could probably start with trying 'menu' or 'settings' or something." Gil shrugged.

"Okay I'll try later. So what's the plan now?"

"Well, I still have to report about my last mission, which was a total failure. But I found you, so I guess that gives me brownie points."

"What was your mission?"

"Well, people have been going missing, probably being captured by the Darkist, but we've been retaliating in kind. Most of my missions are to intercept Darkist patrols and scatter their scouts. I drop them off in well populated areas,

70

erase their memories, and let them find their own way home. This last mission though, it was a complete flop." he sighed. "This particular patrol was comprised of mainly guards not scouts, and they were expecting attack. I had just entered the city when they realized I was there. I barely made it out after they cornered me. Then I ran into you and you know the rest."

"Where was the patrol?"

"Planet Four. I know," he rolled his eyes at her admonishing expression. "But my superior promised some new tech if I went. Actually now that I think about it, they had a few prisoners with them; one of looked them like your uncle according to the picture you showed me and there was a Portalshroom with him."

"Was he okay?" she asked anxiously.

"Well he was unconscious at the time, but he didn't look too beat up."

"That's good. Maybe they took him to Robert."

"Possibly. I recognized one of the guards as Dare Ruin. He's pretty high up in rank but prefers to hang with the lower ranks. He's really popular, originally a Four draft and according to our intel, he's also Robert's guard. If he gets his way, your uncle will probably end up with his brother."

"That's good, right?"

"At least it'll make rescue easier."

"Speaking of rescue, how are we going to get onto Four?"

"The Transporters aren't affected by the Forcefield so we can get on and off, the only problem is Transporters can only move one person so you can't really use them for rescue. Recon missions, personal vacations, shopping sprees- sure why not."

"Wait, then how did Katie, Jake and I get out of her hideout? And back in the cave- how would you have gotten us out if I didn't have a Transporter?"

"It must have been the Portal Crystals she had there, maybe the range was amplified? Same goes for the cave, but instead the energy would have been coming off of you. You did kinda explode. I'd say that warrants a certain amount of energy."

"Oh. Okay."

"Yeah but back on topic, I'd suggest you stay off Four seeing as the Darkist are looking for you. It might be counterproductive if you got captured. We've got evidence that Robert is making some kind of thought reader on Darkist orders so it's now imperative that we not let anyone else get captured."

"So we have to be sneaky?"

"Right, Robert has a Transporter, but obviously he doesn't have it with him. Best case scenario, he hid it before the Darkist got there."

"So we just need to go find it?" Neither of them tried to think of the worst case.

"Yeah. That's it. We could send a message to Dare..." Gil said slowly and frowned staring off into space.

"But he's Darkist."

"He's Four. Doesn't really like the Darkist, and may be willing to help us get a message to your family."

"Think so?" she asked hopefully. "What about Katie and them?"

"Oh yeah," Gil smirked. "They called. They're on their way here."

✪ ✪ ✪

"SLOW DOWN!!" Arya was holding tight to the armrests. "YOU'RE GOING TO KILL US!"

"Relax, I'm one of the best pilots in the ZΣЯΘs! I can drive anything- perfect record at safely crashing things." Katie laughed.

"WHAT?"

"Relax Arya." Lester grinned. "It'll be over that much quicker. The faster she drives, the faster we'll get there."

"And the higher chance she'll kill us!"

"Or the Darkist start chasing us," Ben added helpfully.

"Relax, this craft can out strip anything the Darkist can throw at us." Katie said, increasing the speed slightly to prove her point.

"Just get us there." Arya closed her eyes and held tighter.

"Sure thing, your highness. Lester, does this thing have a shortcut drive."

"Shortcut drive?"

"Any way to take a shortcut through dimensions, instead of going the long way around?"

"Uh... I don't know, it's not my ship."

"You stole it?"

"Borrowed! I *borrowed* it."

"Uh huh right. Don't suppose there's a manual?"

"He lost it the last time." Arya groaned.

"Great. I guess I'll just keep pressing buttons until I find the right one." Katie said unconcerned.

"Try the orange triangle," Ben smiled.

She did and a destinations menu came up. She typed in the super-secret code the R&R used in place of a dimension name and hit the button. A second later they popped into the right dimension.

"Now we just have to figure out where we are and head in the right direction." Katie said smugly.

"This is going to take a while," Ben muttered. "Last time Lester knocked out the navigation system."

Arya tried not to smash something.

✪ ✪ ✪

It was around two in the afternoon when Dare came in. Robert looked up from his work and Jake put his magazine down. The guard looked slightly excited, and passed the inventor a folded piece of paper. Robert glanced over it and nodded before going to the table and picking up some sketches for a random project. Dare motioned for Jake to follow and the three left the room. Once outside, the two brothers followed Dare down the passageway in the direction of the conference room.

Halfway there Dare suddenly stopped and slammed Robert into the wall, causing him to drop his papers. Jake stared and started to move forward angrily, but a glare from the cornered man halted his steps. Dare whispered something to Robert and received an answer. He nodded and drew back, smiling tightly and motioned for them to continue.

At the door to the conference room Dare nodded and stood waiting outside as the two went inside. Jake looked back as the doors were closing and saw Dare wink at him. He turned his attention to the front of the room. Robert had already started his report. Jade was pointedly ignoring the inventor and looking at him instead. He felt like that sharp gaze was looking right through him. He shivered looking out the windows, at the coffee machine, the floor- anything other than her eyes.

"Thank you, Robert." She said, smoothly interrupting him. "That will be all. You may go now. Jake, you stay here." His brother looked at him, raised his eyebrows and shrugged, and gathered his things. He left the room in a hurry, distractedly. Whatever Dare had told him, caused a small smile to appear on his face. Jake only ever saw that smile when he talked about Starlight.

Turning his attention back to the Commander, he steeled himself and met her gaze. "Yes?"

"Jake, in this room I have control of all surveillance and it's currently turned off." She held up a hand to stop his questions. "Just listen. You raised Starlight, you know her. You know she's not going to stop looking for you. Dare had recently gotten a message from the R&R- relayed by Starlight. I, as a Darkist leader, am under orders to apprehend her and all those aiding her. Now you can see what kind of position that puts me in. I don't want to turn my brother in, nor do I want to be accused of aiding the enemy. Now," she crossed her arms.

"Starlight specifically asked Dare about you. I'm afraid I can't give you the context of the message, but I will tell you that she wants Dare or you to find Robert's old Transporter. She wants you to get out of here and is trying to find a way to facilitate a rescue. She's working with the R&R now. My question to you is, have you noticed any character flaws in her? Is she reckless? Arrogant? I need to know."

Seeing the distrust in his eyes, she continued. "I joined the Darkist of my own free will. I agreed with their ideals. When I first encountered them, I was young and they were just the sort of thing I was into at the time. Glory, fame, and a chance to do something about the corrupt governments and laws. I was easily taken in and persuaded."

"But..." Jake acknowledged.

"But they changed. Or rather I was finally able to see them for what they are. Erak doesn't just want to take over and destroy the political side of things, he's insane- mentally unstable, and wants to destroy *everything*. He thinks the only way to fix the ZΣЯΘs is to completely destroy it."

"But nothing has the sheer amount of power to do tha... He wants to use Portal Crystals to..." Jake trailed off as the realization hit full force.

"Yes. He wants to return the ΖΣЯΘs to darkness so he can redo everything 'correctly'," she said. "His OCD has finally gotten the better of him. He's gone over the edge."

"So where do I come into all this?"

"I need you to help my brother and yours to escape before Robert finishes that mind invention of his. The Darkist can't get a hold of this information."

"So don't tell Robert."

"Exactly. I've given you clearance to go anywhere on the planet as long as you have a guard- Dare- with you. Find that Transporter, see if your brother can increase the number of people it can transport and get out of here. Warn Starlight. I don't know if she'll do anything she'd regret later."

"What about you? If they find out what you're doing-"

"I'm prepared for the risks. It's an occupational hazard. The cameras come back on in fifteen seconds, you'd better be gone by then. Dismissed."

Jake nodded and left the room. He had to find Dare ASAP.

CHAPTER 12

"Ease it over, steady... steady... careful!"

"Shut up Arya! I've got this." Katie growled. She carefully steered the craft over the floating pad and away from the water. Slowly but surely the thing inched its way closer to the surface. The craft settled heavily down onto the landing pad. The man directing their flight looked very relived. As they all got out, he remarked, "That's probably the best landing I've ever seen you do, Katie."

"Thanks Scott, I'm getting better."

"Right, so who are your friends?" Scott had long black spiky hair and his long purple bangs covered half his face. He had a little goatee and and eye patch under his hair. The only visible eye had a scar running across it. Goggles sitting on top of his head and a sword on his back completed the look of a daredevil.

"This is Lester, Ben, and- ARYA! LOOK OUT FOR THE SHNORKELFOOSE!"

"The *what*?"

Scott dashed over and pulled the princess away from the edge of the pad. Something big swam just below the surface.

"A shnorkelfoose. Shnorkelfooses look like giant eels, hunt in packs of 5 to 20, and their mouths have several rows of titanium teeth that crunch through spaceships like butter."

Scott told her. "Plus they have an anti-gravity coating on their skin that allows them to jump up and take a bite out of anything flying above. They'll eat anything that moves."

"So why don't they attack the buildings?"

"Shnorkelfoose repellent. The habitats are coated with it. Basically heavy duty diamond juice."

"Right that makes *so* much sense." Arya scoffed.

"Whatever, it's true. This planet is entirely covered with water and the only places to land are these pads. Over there are the habitats," he pointed.

The habitats looked like giant floating bubbles with mini cities inside. There were inflated tunnels connecting them and it all had a distinctly futuristic feel to it. "Wow," Ben grinned. "You guys sure were right about the R&R having good tech."

"And food!" Lester added.

"Starlight and Gil are expecting you. They're in the gym at the moment but I'll call them out." Scott messed with the watch on his wrist, sending a message. "Now if you'll follow me, we can get you rooms and meet your friends in the mess hall."

"Come on guys!" Katie started after him. "Today is Friday, all-you-can-eat buffet day!"

"FOOD!" Lester grinned.

Starlight looked up from her food staring at the doors. "Why do I feel like someone is going to come in here and slap me?"

"Don't worry, I'll protect you," Gil laughed. "No one is going to slap you."

"Still..." She grumbled. "Oh look, here come the cavalry."

The pair watched as Katie and company walked in led by Gil's friend Scott. "Gil! I've brought the people you asked me to meet."

"Thanks Scott. Hey Katie, didn't think I'd see you around here anytime soon." Gil laughed.

"Yeah well, some people came and lost me my hideout to the Darkist," she glared at Starlight, "And these weirdos I've got with me needed a lift."

"Well, nice to meet you weirdos. I'm Gil. You're Lester and Arya right? I think I've seen you here a coupla times, but *you* I've never seen." He gave Ben a onceover raising his eyebrow.

"He's my boyfriend." Arya said coolly.

"I'm Ben. Nice to meet you."

"Hi, so you guys wanna get some food and then we'll talk?"

"Sounds good!" Lester rubbed his hands together.

Once everyone was settled, Gil started the discussion. "Okay, so here's the rundown. We all know what shape the R&R leadership is in, so we'll have to do everything ourselves off the books. Now, Robert Gilgalad is in the process of making something for the Darkist that can basically read thoughts. The R&R wants him back before he can. Jake, his brother, and a guard called Dare have agreed to help us get him out. They're looking for Robert's old Transporter as a backup plan to get him off Planet Four. The idea on our end was to attempt an extraction rescue. Have someone here with a Transporter take an extra and grab him."

"Yeah," Starlight interrupted. "But if we do that, Jake will still be stuck there. We'd need two people with two extra Transporters to get them both out. And if we wanted to get Dare out too we'd need one person with three... But we only have three here, so they'd still need to find Robert's old one."

"Wouldn't it just be easier to sneak in with a Darkist supply unit through the open portals?" Katie asked.

"Possibly," Gil mused. "But what if we got caught? To avoid that, we'd need a team of Blenders and we only have two."

"You have Blenders here?" Ben asked in awe.

"Yeah, and you're looking right at them." Gil grinned, putting a hand on Starlight's shoulder. The amazed looks they got from the others were priceless. "Let me introduce, Princess Star of Atlantis and Gillian... the Annoying." he crossed his arms smugly.

"The Annoying? Really?" Katie shook her head. "If she's from Atlantis, then she's *way* older than you."

"So? At the moment she's sixteen and I'm nineteen."

"I have to break up the party," Arya rolled her eyes. "But how does this relate to our problem?"

"Oh, uh well..." Gil cleared his throat. "Right- all Darkist checkpoints have DNA scanners, they won't let you through unless you're cleared. So Star and I would have to replace a couple of 'em. That would work going in-"

"But going out, we'd still need the Transporters," Starlight cut in. "They're not cleared to leave," she shrugged.

"But if we had a distraction..." Gil looked at Scott.

"And someone on the inside," Starlight added. "One of us could take Robert's place so they wouldn't realize he's gone until it's too late."

"Still needs a lot of planning." Arya said skeptically. "But it's a good start."

"Then we'd better get to work." Gil said.

"Anybody need some material for more Transporters?" Katie asked with a grin.

✪ ✪ ✪

Erak frowned. "Joshua, any word from the scavengers?"

"No Sir. Not yet."

"And the Crystals from Boardo's hideout?"

"No trace. However we've gathered some readings from one of our old ships."

"Weren't those supposed to be destroyed?" Erak asked irritably.

"They were. Although I'm sure pirates scavenged some of the pieces off. The readings were from one of the old navigation systems. It sent out a signal that it had been damaged."

"So where is it?" Erak demanded. He ran his hand through his perfectly slicked back black hair.

"We don't know- yet. We're tracking it as we speak. All the other parts taken from the old ships must have been destroyed or disabled. Whoever took this bit must not have been too bright."

"That, or it's a decoy. Take care of it."

"Yes sir. Anything else?"

"Inform Jade that I'll be visiting Four next week. Routine inspection."

"Yes Sir."

"And Joshua? Straighten your ribbons, they're off centered."

✪ ✪ ✪

"Right. We have four basic Transporters, programmed to take the user to one of our other bases near here. That way if anyone tries to get their hands on them, they won't be taken straight to HQ," Katie said triumphantly. The group was gathered on the landing pad. "Only a few people know how to make a proper Transporter, so it wasn't easy let me tell you."

"Good, and the fake profiles?" Arya asked. She had taken over command of their little group and everyone was perfectly happy to take orders from the victorious war veteran. As a royal, her time in the wars on her home planet was expected and she rose to the challenge with determination. Most of her skill came from outmaneuvering her enemies and her tactics were unparalleled. The R&R had recruited her after her retirement. Which was probably a good thing considering their leadership. Gil had half a mind to let her take over, consequences be damned.

"Ready and so integrated into their system that they won't be able to find anything wrong with them." Katie grinned.

"Extraction team?"

"We're ready." Gil said. "Starlight's got a perfect memory when it comes to details. Ben already has soldier training and I trust Scott not to mess anything up."

"Good. Katie will stay here for tech support and Lester and I will meet you at the pickup point. This is an in and out mission. No side vendettas people. If you run into trouble don't be heroic. I need you all back here."

"Yes ma'am." Gil nodded. "Alright team, let's move out. If you get separated from the group or we run into trouble, use your Transporter and get out of there."

They nodded and boarded the commandeered high tech R&R ship. Katie waved them off and retreated from the engines' range. "Everyone's earpiece and mic work?" she asked.

Sounds of affirmation were heard through their secure line. "Good. Once you're in, I'll walk you through it. Until then, have a nice ride. I've programed the correct route into the ship so you don't have to worry about getting lost."

The spacecraft continued to rapidly ascend from the pad, quickly getting out of Shnorkelfoose range. It soon entered the upper atmosphere and left the planet behind. The speed was incredible, outstripping the ship they came in by leagues. The ride was so smooth you couldn't tell they were moving except by the way the stars zipped past them, similar to watching raindrops fly past while driving.

About two hours into their flight, they slowed and entered the atmosphere of another planet. This time the craft didn't descend to the surface, instead landing on a spaceport high in the sky.

"Well, looks like this is our stop," Arya said. "Good luck and don't do anything stupid."

"Come back, preferably alive." Lester added, grinning.

"Will do, if possible." Gil said. "Try not to get too bored while we're gone." The doors closed and the engines started back up. "Hold tight guys. These things can go *really* fast. Lightspeed is nothing." True to his word, they were soon flying faster than any of them had ever been, and Starlight had been to some *pretty* high speeds.

"So how long until we get to the nearest Darkist supply route?" Ben asked.

"Well, at this speed about five hours. We have to take the long way around, seeing as this thing doesn't have a shortcut drive, which are technically speaking, illegal."

"But illegal is faster."

"True, but for this operation, we need to time everything perfectly. If we could take a shortcut there, there's no telling where we'd end up. It would put us in the right dimension but probably not near our destination."

"So like going if you wanted to travel cross country, let's say New York to LA, it would take me to California but some random place in California." Starlight asked.

"Pretty much," Gil nodded.

"Where's California?" Ben asked.

"It's on Earth dummy," Scott said. "So Starlight, what are you doing after this?"

"Not interested." She crossed her arms.

"Dang it. You got a boyfriend or something?"

"No. Just not interested."

"Woah, burn!" Ben grinned. "She got you there Scott."

"So is this how guys occupy their time?" Starlight raised her eyebrows.

"Only when there's a pretty lady and a lot of time." Scott laughed.

"Well thanks. This is going to be a long ride isn't it. Its times like these that I wish I could channel my inner Arya."

"Oh please don't," Ben said dramatically.

"So, you and Arya?"

"It's an arranged thing." The elf sighed.

"Oh, but you seem to like her."

"Yeah, but she's got a nasty temper."

"I can agree with that." Starlight laughed. "Even the air around her turned red at the party."

"Yeah but she's great once you get to know her."

"Voluntarily or through forced contact."

"Eh... She holds grudges for a very long time."

"Ah, so don't get on her bad side?"

"She and Lester are really close, and he's known for being the worst trickster around. So if you piss her off, good luck. She's scary, but he'll steal your pride."

"Duly noted." They lapsed into silence and Ben soon fell asleep. Starlight decided to follow his example and closed her eyes.

✪ ✪ ✪

Blue. Everything was blue. It was the first thing she became aware of. She didn't have a name for it at the time, but soon she assigned the thing she was seeing with a color. Blue and a tingly feeling. She didn't know it- at the time she didn't know anything- but she was changing, evolving, the blue tingles targeted her cells pouring into her DNA. Soon it was replaced with the blue tingles. It didn't hurt exactly, seeing as her nerves hadn't yet formed, but she could feel the tingles all the same. Her brain, not fully formed, couldn't process anything yet; but her soul could. It was green- or green was the closest thing she was later able to associate the feeling with. Green, not blue. Strange.

Over the next indeterminable period of time- she later learned it was about seven months- she floated in her small world and listened. The most frequent voice she heard was a female- safety. The other prevalent voice was male- protection. There were other voices too, but fainter, farther away. She learned that the female was called Mother and the male Father. She learned to recognize the voices and her mind recorded everything they said even if she didn't understand it.

Soon the space she was in vanished and a bright light assaulted her eyes. The noises were louder and she recognized the voice called Nurse. "Why isn't she crying? What's wrong with her?"

"Her eyes are open and she's breathing normally enough," the one called Doctor said.

"She's beautiful," said Mother. "Look at her eyes, they're bright violet."

"Neither you or your husband have that dark a skin tone," Nurse said. "And her hair is pure white."

"She's special," Mother said softly.

"It's probably from that encounter with the Portal Crystals, you highness." Doctor said. His voice was the loudest. "Do you have a name for her yet?"

"Star." That voice was Father's. "We're naming her Star."

"Because she shines like a star." Mother said proudly.

Star giggled. They all looked at her. "She is the strangest baby I've ever seen." Doctor said.

Star just smiled. She knew she was special, everyone had always told her so. She latched onto her mother and closed her eyes.

Starlight woke with a start. Memories had been plaguing her dreams all week, ever since she first got her memories back. She looked over at her companions. Gil was staring at the readout on the screen, Ben was reading, and Scott was busy with some game. Gil looked up and said, "We're here."

CHAPTER 13

They landed in a busy port, traffic coming and going, including the Darkist shipment they were after. They docked the ship and headed out onto the pier. The manager came over and said, "Its 30$_z$'s to dock your craft here." Z's, the inter-dimensional currency of the ΖΣЯΘs. Gil handed over the proper amount. "What name shall I put it under?" the manager asked. He was an orange alien, with several tentacles and bat like wings.

"Gilbert," Gil replied.

"Welcome to the Zilos Spaceport Mr. Gilbert. Enjoy your stay."

"Thank you, come on guys." Gil led the way through the maze of piers and docks and into the main part of the port. It looked like a steampunk city, all metal and gears, mixed with sleek white and silver space age technology, interspersed with odd glowing bits here and there. It was a bizarre mix but it blended seamlessly together and looked as if it belonged.

"The Darkist caravan will get here in about an hour." Gil said. "So you have less than that to get into costume and get to your stations. Then we need to apprehend the Darkist soldiers we'll be replacing. You two," he indicated Scott and Ben. "Are posing as pickups. All you have to do is join the soldiers and find your captain. You already have the info, so don't mess this up. Try to be as inconspicuous as possible.

If you get into trouble, use your Transporter. Now split up, I'll see you all on Planet Four."

The four of them parted ways and Starlight entered the nearest pub, going straight for the restrooms. She changed into the Darkist uniform Lester had provided, still wondering where he'd gotten his hands on it, and looked in the mirror. Concentrating, she watched as her features changed into that of young man with blonde hair and hazel eyes. Hadley Wilson was his name, a mid-rank Darkist soldier bound for her home planet. He wasn't especially handsome, but definitely not ugly. He was a slightly shy soul, so her job shouldn't be too hard.

Being male felt as comfortable as female to her, so she took it in stride. She'd posed as males often enough to know how they worked. She left the restroom, bought herself a drink, sat down in a corner to wait, her face covered slightly by the hair hanging in front of her eyes. Pouring her drink into the plant next to her, she raised the near empty cup to her lips every now and then. Now was definitely not the time to get drunk. Soon the Darkist arrived and went on break. She had another hour to blend in and find her ship before they left.

Giving herself another fifteen minutes, Starlight stood and exited the establishment. *Show time*, she thought. *Okay, I need pier number nine, dock seven. It should be the third ship down.* Locating the right one, she kept an eye out for the real Hadley. She walked into the ship and looked around. One of the seats was labeled Wilson, H. She walked over and opened the bag at her feet, pretending to add something.

"Hadley, that was fast."

The voice took her off guard but she didn't show it. "Yeah, I did my business and came back. Don't really want to lose track of time and get left here." She replied zipping the bag back up. She turned to meet the man addressing her. Luckily it seemed to be in character.

"Do me a favor and go find Lione. You know how he is in bars."

"Yessir." She turned and left the ship. *Find Hadley and this Lione person. Dispose of Hadley, bring back Lione. Right, where the heck are they?*

She wandered around, sending out a silent probe. As they were able to change their DNA, Blenders had to be able to differentiate between themselves, other Blenders, and anyone else. They'd do so using Soulforce. Soulforce was basically someone's being or aura. Every living thing has Soulforce whether or not it has a soul, including anything from humans to grass to bacteria. So Starlight scanned the Soulforce in her general area, looking for Hadley and Lione.

She found Hadley in a bar down the street, Lione was a few streets over. She quickly changed her facial features to avoid recognition and ducked inside. Hadley was sitting with some friends and just getting up to use the restroom. *Perfect*, she thought. Following, she entered through the door a few minutes after him. He was just washing his hands when she came in. Locking the door behind her. He heard the click and looked up nervously. She smiled at him and moved towards the sink.

"L-look," he stuttered. "I don't want any trouble. We have to leave soon and-"

"Relax Hadley, I'm not going to mug you."

"You're not?" he looked relieved but suspicious.

"No, I'm just going to wipe your memory and take your place." She grinned and hit him hard on the head. He didn't even have time to throw up his hands. She caught him as he fell and carried him to the farthest stall, setting him down on the toilet. Luckily they look somewhat similar to the ones on Earth. Shooting him with Gil's memory gun, she locked the stall. Her form turned to goo and slipped under the low door. A quick look in the mirror told her that she looked like Hadley again. She suddenly remembered how much she loved field work.

She waved to his friends and said, "Well, I've got to go find Lione. You know how he is in bars." They all laughed and turned back to their conversation. Starlight headed back outside and followed her internal compass to her charge. He was sitting at the counter surrounded by a mixed group of females and seemed to be in the midst of telling some dramatic story in which he was the hero. She could clearly make out his name tag, Brian Lione, and headed over.

"Well, well... If it isn't the magnificent Brian Lione!" She said. "Hello ladies."

"Hadley! I was just telling these fine ladies here about my many adventures."

"Misadventures more likely. I was sent to find you so you don't miss your next escapade!" She told the ladies in a stage whisper, "Considering how he is in bars. Come on now Brian, the ship leaves in fifteen minutes with or without you."

"Now, now Hadley! Don't spoil our fun!"

"Personally, I don't care if you stay here. I'd rather stay here actually, but we don't get paid until we get to Four, and I'd rather not drink myself into poverty in this fine establishment."

"Well, you hear the man ladies, until next time." Lione grinned. He and Starlight left the building with the women giggling after them. "Hadley, I didn't know you had it in you! You're usually the more silent type."

"True enough," Starlight quickly scanned the other man's memories. "But I've been working on 'coming out of my shell' like you said."

"Well, you certainly made an impression back there, keep it up and I might actually have some real competition."

"Let's just get back to the ship."

"And there's the Hadley we all know! Spoilsport."

Starlight rolled her eyes and led the way. Fifteen minutes later the Darkist ships left the Zilos Spaceport and she was on her way.

Over the next few days they passed several checkpoints without any trouble. The scanners read her DNA as Hadley Wilson and didn't complain. The Darkist ships went noticeably slower than the ship they came in, and around noon on the third day they entered the Terminal Solar System. From there they would take a portal to Planet Four. Scanning through the final outside checkpoint, Starlight and her shipmates unloaded their cargo onto the hover trolleys. Their destination, the Hall of Portals.

Stepping through the swirling blue screen, Starlight had her first glimpse of Planet Four in sixteen years. All the Portals here were much bigger than the one she'd been working on in her basement. The Hall of Portals looked very empty with most of the gates closed and void of citizen traffic with only a few Darkist guards standing around. It used to be the center of travel and trade in the ZΣЯƟs. Now it was just another abandoned station. Designed similar to an Earth airport, the Hall of Portals had two-way portals to all major regions in ZΣЯƟs. Tunnels led off into the different wings to terminals, connecting each specific region. Within the terminals, were all the portals to each sector. Each region was in charge of the rate of travel to their sectors. Like an airport, you could accompany someone that was taking a Portal to the security check-in but no further. Those checkpoints being each regional area. But now only Darkist approved traffic went in and out, and with the Darkist monitoring all portal activity there could be no unauthorized traveling. All the Portals were powered by the Portal Stone energy, same as the city. When the Atlanteans had moved the city, their Portals Stones came with them. Buried deep within the bowels of Kapital city, they were the main power source for everything on Four. They still had the biggest collection of portal stones in the ΖΣЯΘs, which was why the Darkist had made it a priority to occupy Four.

Starlight inwardly sighed and followed the cargo out into the city, heading for the warehouses. There she would duck into an alley to meet with the rest of her team and Dare, who had promised that the cameras would be turned off there.

Waving to her shipmates she said, "Well, I'm going to take the rest of the day off. See you guys tomorrow." Then she headed for the alley. Everyone was already there, and so far the plan had gone off without a hitch. She changed back to herself and joined them.

"Starlight, you're here. Good. Okay, remember the plan. Scott and I will go after Jake, Starlight and Ben will go after Robert. Starlight, you're replacing Robert. Dare, make it look like you took Jake out for a break. Any progress on Robert's Transporter?" Gil asked.

"Not yet. Jake had been asking Robert questions about his old inventions. He says he doesn't remember where he left it, which is good so the Darkist don't find it, but bad cause we need it. Jake didn't want to push it in case Robert got suspicious." Dare said.

"Okay, so we have your sister in on this right?" Gil asked.

"Yes, although she has plausible deniability." Dare laughed. "By the way, we might have a problem... Erak Darke is visiting for a routine inspection, and he kinda had this thing for Jade. So there's no way to contact her all week without alerting anyone. The appropriate cameras will be turned off at the right time, but she won't be actively helping us."

"Roger that. Alright people, let's go."

Starlight nodded and turned invisible, following Dare back to Robert's workshop. The other three went to the mall to wait for Dare and Jake. "Okay, be careful Star. There's cameras everywhere beyond this alley. So don't become visible for any reason. I'll let you know when we do the switch."

"Right," she whispered. They left the alley and reentered the city. After a short walk from the warehouse district they came to the City Hall, where they were holding Robert. She silently followed Dare through the maze of passageways and stepped onto the Telepad after him. Her first glimpse of her adoptive father was an odd one. He was leaning over back on an exercise ball fiddling with the underside of some kind of machine and grumbling to himself.

"Robert," Dare said announcing his presence. "I need to talk to you for a minute."

The inventor waved his foot in acknowledgment and continued doing whatever he was doing. Starlight glanced around and saw the top of a familiar head poking over the top of the couch.

"Hey Jake," Dare grinned. "You in the mood for food?"

"Food?" Jake turned around quickly and grinned at the guard.

"Yeah, mall food."

"FOOD!" Jake said triumphantly. "Robby, want me to bring back anything?"

"Get me some of that chicken stuff you got last time," Robert said. Rolling to a sitting position on the ball. "That was good. You wanted to talk to me Dare?"

"I don't know if anyone told you, but Erak Darke is here," the guard said. "He might want to come see what you're working on, so..."

"Clean up?"

"Yeah..." The room was a mess of tools, materials, and blueprints that only made sense to the inventor. "That'd probably be a good idea," Dare nodded. "Plus Jade wants you to report before he finds her and sticks to her. Field trip!"

"Yeah okay. Just let me get my stuff."

The three of them- four including their invisible escort- left the room. In the same hallway Dare had slammed Robert against the wall, he slowed. "Now, would be a good time..." he whispered. Starlight pressed the extra Transporter into Robert's hand who jumped slightly at the unseen contact.

"Hey Dad," Starlight whispered. "Hold tight." He vanished without a trace. Jake stared astonished. "Play it cool, Jake. It's a rescue op."

"Sta-"

"SHH!" She reappeared looking exactly like Robert. "Okay, let's go. He's out."

Dare suddenly put a hand to his earpiece. "Right, Jade changed her mind, you don't have to report. Field trip canceled."

The newly replaced Robert winked at his 'brother'. "Have fun at the mall."

Dare watched as the inventor reentered his workshop. "Come on, your turn."

✪ ✪ ✪

Robert's world had turned to a storm of pain. He was vaguely aware of a sharp zap on the back of his neck and braced himself for the wave of pain that always followed. It didn't come. He frowned. *What?* He opened his eyes and saw a face with silver eyes staring back at him.

"Hello Robert. You're safe. Your tracking devices have been disabled. The Darkist can't find you. Try to wake up."

"What...?" he croaked.

"My name is Arya. Your daughter just rescued you. You're safe."

"My- Star?"

"Yes. Drink this and then you can go back to sleep. The others will be here soon."

"Okay."

✪ ✪ ✪

Starlight yawned. She had been pretending to mess around with Robert's inventions for the cameras. She lazily stood up and walked over to the couch, falling onto it and closing her eyes. Someone appeared on the telepad and entered the room. "Jake, did you get my chicken?"

No one answered and she cracked her eyes open. Erak Darke was glaring down at her. "Hello Star, trying to make a mess of things again are you?"

CHAPTER 14

Robert opened his eyes. He was lying on something soft. The room he was in was dim, but enough light shone through the windows to see. There weren't proper walls but curtains, looking like some kind of hospital or infirmary. The walls were a sleek glossy white and electric blue lights shone through the open door. His head ached but other than that he felt fine. Slowly sitting up, he stretched, yawned and rubbed the back of his neck. There was nothing there. Frowning, he sat up straight, feeling for the device that had been there for the past sixteen years.

"We've removed all Darkist surveillance from you." He looked up and saw Arya standing by an opening in the curtains.

"Thank you. Who are you? Or actually who are you with?"

"The R&R, but this mission wasn't approved by them. Actually they didn't know it was happening. It was Starlight's idea."

"Starlight? My Star?"

"Star, Starlight, whatever. The Blender chick. The only problem is she's currently MIA."

"What?"

"She was supposed to replace you for a while to make sure you got away. She hasn't reported yet and it's been three days. The other part of the team, including your brother all made it back."

"Jake is here? Where is... here?"

"One of the R&R spaceports. About two hours away from headquarters." Arya opened the light blue curtains over the windows. Light flooded in and Robert was able to see her properly. She was dressed in the black skintight R&R uniform with a silver breastplate, a trio of dark green belts slung across her right hip over a white piece of fabric tied on her left hip. She had on a pair of dark grey mid-calf boots with white straps. Completing the outfit was a flowing white cape.

"What's with the get up?"

"Unfortunately the Darkist managed to track the others back. They know we're here. So far there's been no attacks, but we're expecting one. And until they do, we're stuck waiting."

"Is there anything I can do to help?"

"Well... There may be one thing."

"Are you sure this is a good idea?" Lester said nervously. He was standing on the edge of the white round landing pad with about three miles of empty air beneath him. "What if it doesn't work?"

"It'll work, I made it." Robert crossed his arms. "Well, go ahead. Jump off."

"Don't worry," Gil laughed. "If you fall, I'll catch you. I've got plenty of time to." The green haired Blender was currently equipped with a pair of angel-like wings the same shade as his hair.

"Why can't you make something more organic like *his* wings?" Lester grumbled.

"He's a Blender, and I'm more of a mechanic than a biologist." Robert grinned. "Go on, try 'em out."

Lester closed his eyes and shook his head. "No!"

"Should I give him a push?" Arya asked.

"What?! No- wait you can't- ahhhhhh!" Lester screamed as his sister pushed him off the edge.

"Hit the button when you're ready," Robert yelled after him.

"Should I go comfort him?" Gil smirked.

"Might as well."

Gil grinned and took a running start off the pad. He lept majestically into the air, struck a heroic pose and plummeted towards the ground. Then his wings caught the air as he shot upwards. Flashing the spectators a grin, he rode the air currents to where Lester was still falling. "Push the button!" he yelled over the wind, gesturing to the on button by Lester's thumb.

Lester frantically pressed it, but nothing happened. He gave Gil an it's-not-working look and continued to panic. "The other button!" Gil rolled his eyes. Lester pressed the other button and the results were immediate. From the small rig on Lester's back, two wings sprouted. They were transparent and glowed blue, slicing through the air and holding his body aloft. Shaped similar to dragonfly wings, they were designed for speed. Once Lester got over the shock of flying, he and Gil were soon racing through the air.

"This is aaamaaazing!" Lester yelled.

"And you didn't want to try it!" Gil teased.

"Yes I did, I just didn't want it not to work!"

"Well it's working now!" Gil laughed. "The button you were pressing was to pull the wings back in. Come on, let's go back up. They'll want a report."

"Right, race you!"

"You're on!"

Lester's wings won the race for speed but Gil was much more used to flying than the elf. They both settled back down onto the landing pad and Lester retracted the wings. "This is great! Best birthday present ever!"

"You're welcome," Arya grinned.

"How's it handle?" Robert asked.

"Like a dream. I've always wanted to fly!" Lester grinned.

The boys went back out and Arya turned to the inventor. "How's Jake?"

"Still worried about Starlight. I keep telling him that she's been fine for billions of years, so she'll be fine for a few days. She's smart that one. I'm sure she'll get herself out of there sooner or later, she always does."

❂ ❂ ❂

I need to get out of here, Starlight thought. *But I need to sabotage something first... but what? What big plans do the Darkist have?* She looked over at the cell across from hers. Dare was asleep. How was a mystery. His wrists were shackled to the ceiling, the chain holding him on tiptoe. It must have been extremely uncomfortable, but there was no way to help him. She could easily walk through the shield containing her, but the cell would recognize it was unoccupied and the guns trained on Dare would fire.

Should have known they'd use a living shield, she thought angrily. *They know they can't contain me. I can't even use my Transporter without him dying.* "Erak!" she yelled in frustration. "Erak!"

Right... save Dare, get out of here... not necessarily in that order. She frowned, *It's like a giant puzzle. I can contact people with my Transporter, but the video cameras are watching. I could send interference... but they might shoot him if the feed is messed up.*

Rubbing her head, Starlight felt the signs of a headache coming on. *Interference... Interference... I've got it!* She

grinned, *Dimensional interference! But how to cause it?*
The grin fell from her face. *Come on, think!* She reviewed
her memories from the time Erak caught her to the present.

"*Hello Star, trying to make a mess of things again
are you?*"

*She looked up at the Darkist leader and smiled, dropping
her disguise.* "*You weren't suppose to find out yet. Oh well.*"

"*Good to know. Guess what we found at the mall?*"

"*Your conscience?*"

He ignored her quip and continued, "*A certain guard.
He was helping some people to escape. By the way, I
didn't know you had entered into the profession of making
Transporters.*"

"*I haven't, that would be Katie Boardo. I believe your
guys invaded her hideout.*"

"*Yes and you know what we didn't find?*"

"*Your better half?*"

"*Where did you take the Portal Stones?*"

"*I don't know what you're talking about Erak,*" *her voice
was sickly sweet.*

"*I'm sure you do. Because you see, this guard is currently
in a cell with about twenty guns pointed at his head. So
unless you want him to get shot, I'd suggest you play along.*"
He took out a holoscreen and showed her the footage.

"*For the sake of your manly pride, I'll comply. But I'm
warning you. I don't know him. You can only hold this over
me for so long, before I decide he's not worth it.*"

"*Then he'll die.*"

"*People die all the time, what do I care?*"

"*He saved your uncle.*"

"*That's my uncle's problem not mine. Your point?*"

"*But you* are *playing along, so he must mean* something
to you."

"I'm only here because I want to be. Remember that Erak."

After that encounter, she had been escorted to her lovely cell and left alone. Maybe they thought she'd refrain from doing anything if they didn't talk to her. "Yeah right," she mumbled under her breath. If there was some way to get her Transporter to Dare...

The brunette groaned and blinked, his muscles sore and stiff. "Hey," he croaked and gave a half effort at a grin. "What's happening?"

"Nothing at the moment," Starlight sighed. "I'm attempting to think of an escape plan that will leave both of us alive."

"That's probably a good thing." He laughed. "Is there any way to get some water around here?"

"Yeah hang on..." Deciding that water wouldn't trigger the guns, she concentrated and sent a stream of water his way.

"That's not exactly what I meant," he said raising an eyebrow, water streaming from his hair. She grinned and directed the moisture into his skin, hydrating him instantly. "Well, that works I guess," he grinned.

"Hey, I'm sorry for dragging you into this mess."

"Nah, its fine. Occupational hazard and all that. So what's the escape plan?"

"I'll let you know when I've got one." She shrugged.

"Fair enough."

"Okay I've got."

"Well, that was quick." He grinned, "Is it a good one?"

"Well, if we don't end up dead, then yeah I guess so. It involves a water balloon fight, ketchup, and some good old fashioned spy music."

"Alright then, when do we start?"

"We just did."

✪ ✪ ✪

"What is she doing?" Erak asked, irritated.

"Planning an escape, Sir." The two men were standing in the control center.

"I know that! But it's hardly up to her level. Water-balloons? Really?"

"Sir, I doubt that's her actual plan, although playing spy music during an escape is definitely her style." Joshua hid his smile very well.

"Well, get down there and do something!" Erak demanded.

"Yes, Sir." The second in command failed to completely hide his smile that time.

Joshua made his way down through the maze of hallways to the holding cells. Starlight was throwing spurts of water through the shield that made up the walls of the cell, which Dare was catching in his mouth. The two were laughing and ignored the officer's entrance.

"Nice one Star!" Dare grinned, after catching three in a row.

"What are you two doing?" Joshua asked, this time making no effort to hide his amusement.

"Trying to annoy Erak," Starlight smirked. "Obviously it worked."

"What do you want?"

"Ketchup, balloons, and the mission impossible theme on loud speakers."

"Uh huh, and how is that going to improve your condition?"

"It won't, but it'll bother Erak."

"I see." He crossed his arms. "And why should I do what you say?"

"Cause I just brainwashed you." She laughed. "Now bring me my effects, slave!"

Joshua turned and left, grumbling all the while.

"Did you really brainwash him?" Dare asked.

"No, I hypnotized him."

"Really?"

"Yes." *No.* The answer echoed in Dare's head. He blinked, confused. *He just likes seeing Erak pissed off. And yes, I'm actually thinking to you, you're not crazy. Us Blenders can do a lot of cool stuff.*

So I've noticed, Dare thought. *How is it even possible that you exist? Shouldn't the laws of fairness and this-person-is-too-powerful come into effect here?*

There's no such rules, Starlight grinned. *And if there were, then our natural character flaws would balance it out.*

Like what?

Well, I've got what Jake likes to call my 'saving people' thing. I have issues with standing aside and letting people be hurt. Plus I'm legally mentally insane. I've got so many issues you wouldn't even believe.

Like how you tear yourself up when your friends die and you can't?

Starlight froze and looked at him. "Yes." It was barely above a whisper. He could see the pain behind her eyes. He watched as she retreated into herself and closed her eyes. Was she really that easy to read? She knew she was an open book, but the redhead prided herself on her acting skills. All that relative sense of safety on Earth must have made her rusty.

Okay... Plan of escape that includes ketchup and water balloons... Why did I think of that anyway? This has got to be the most stupid escape plan in the history of stupid escape plans. Starlight could feel Dare's pitying gaze on her. She kept her eyes closed.

"Dare," she said aloud. "How do you feel about roller coasters?"

✪ ✪ ✪

"Should I give her what she asked for, Sir?" Joshua said, his voice neutral and controlled. "Most of the recruits here think she's just a legend- an overly exaggerated one at that."

"So we should give them a show? Make sure they know what they're up against?" Erak retorted. "That's all very well, but have *you* forgotten who we're dealing with Commander? I don't want to take the risk."

"Of losing her? Sir if I may, she'll be back. She always comes back, if only to gloat. We have Time on our side, Sir. Control of the Portals alone is more than enough, but with the addition of S-"

"I said never to speak of it! You don't know if she's watching!" Erak snapped.

"With all due respect, I think she's too busy to watch us." Joshua couldn't stop the grin from breaking out.

True to her word, the Mission Impossible song blared out over the speakers. "Damn." Erak pounded a fist on the desk.

"Looks like she acquired her effects without help." Joshua raised an eyebrow. Erak stormed out with a group of heavily armed soldiers. The rest of the room's occupants were glued to the screens. On his way out, Joshua slipped one of the Techies some Z's and grinned. *That should get her back to R&R in no time.*

On screen, Starlight could be seen dramatically sneaking around and throwing ketchup filled water balloons at any unlucky passers by. Dare was simply handing her more ammunition. The paid Techy smiled and pressed a few more buttons for good measure, however the flying laser sharks were a bit much.

"So... now what?" Dare asked. He was still in his cell, guns pointed at his head. Starlight had just asked him about rollercoasters when the loud speakers had started blasting out her request.

"Wait for it... Waaaait for it... Aaaaaand... Juuust about now... Oh come on already!" She frowned. Then there was a flash and Dare was suddenly standing next to her. Across the hall the guns started firing. "Save Dare, check. Get outta here, working on it. Brace yourself. This might get a bit violent," the teen warned.

"Wait what?" Dare barely had time to close his mouth before he felt a sensation similar to Portal travel but more condensed, and suddenly they were standing on the deck of a ship. A pirate ship to be more precise. Full of pirates with sharp and explosive objects. All pointing at them. "Oh," Dare winced. "Right."

CHAPTER 15

Captain Alastor Azazel, the Demon of the Dark, Killer of Dreams, the Nightmare, and most feared pirate in all the ΖΣЯΘs. Strikes without mercy, kills on sight, and also happens to owe a certain redhead his life.

"Alastor!" Starlight grinned. "Long time, no see! So sorry to drop in like this, we were on the run from some Darkist, and you were in a convenient location. You used that shortcut drive I got you, didn't you? Thanks *so* much by the way. You just provided the means for our escape."

"Glad teh help. Stand down men, we wouldn't want teh scare this helpless maiden here," the captain laughed.

"She's not helpless!" Dare protested.

"I was takin' 'bout you, lassie." The crew laughed. "Aye, you're welcome on meh ship anytime, miss Trouble. Who's your friend?"

"Dare... Ruin."

"Ruin!?" he shouted angrily. "Just let meh hands on 'im!" Dare stepped back, alarmed. "I'll have his guts, I will!"

"Starlight?" And if his voice was an octave higher than normal, no one could blame him.

"Relax, Dare. He's just messing with ya."

The captain grinned. "Aww, don't worry lassie, I'd never harm a relation of Jade Ruin. Done me a favor that one 'as.

Good lass. Iron will. People who know which direction is up, 'preciate her work. Double agent an all that."

"Wait what? My sister isn't-"

"Shut up Dare. Alastor, can you give us a ride? We've got a few things we need to round up." Starlight grinned.

"Yeah sure, what's our heading, Trouble?"

The redhead's vampire smile scared even the dread Captain Alastor Azazel.

"So just to be clear, we got here by a combination of your amazing Transporter and some kind of dimensional rift?" Dare summed up. He, Starlight, and the Captain were gathered in the Captain's quarters pouring over maps of the ZΣЯΘs and planning their next step.

"Yes. Whenever a shortcut drive is used, it creates a dimensional rift that allows the craft to move through- the short cut. The fallout from that can be controlled and used in part with a Transporter to transport more than one person," the redhead nodded.

"Aye, an Trouble here calls asking meh teh use meh shortcut drive, didn't care where to, just so long as I used it." Captain Azazel grinned. "So I figured she'd be turnin' up soon."

"My Transporter can search out and recognize energy patterns like dimensional rifts. Lucky for us, I'm starting to remember most of the things I knew about it." Starlight glanced at the necklace. "Its way more powerful than any of the ones Katie made, and outstrips Gil's by light years. Robert is a *very* creative man. Most people wouldn't even think to put half the features he did into his Transporter."

"So we're gonna go pick up a few things and drop yeh of at this spaceport in some random dimension that isn't s'posed teh have anything in it?" the pirate confirmed.

"Yup, and I'd tell you what's in it, but I don't think you want to know old friend."

"Naw, I'm good with the Darkist not interrogating meh."

"Good. In that case, let's get moving," Starlight grinned. She left the cabin with Dare on her heels.

"Why does he call you Trouble?" the brunette asked.

"That's how I was introduced to him and they like to give out literal names here."

"So you're trouble?"

"But of *course!*" She laughed. "I used to be a pirate a few cycles ago, you know. Made a pretty interesting reputation for myself. When Captain Azazel here hears I'm back in business last cycle, well... Let's just say people are afraid of me for a reason."

"So he comes and finds you?"

"No, I'm passing by and he needs a little help with some Darkist. I save his life, he is eternally grateful. Knows I'm something strange, but doesn't know what. Long story short, you can count him as an ally."

"Well, that's good I suppose. But what are you picking up?"

"You'll see. By my guess, the rest of my team will need some help. I took a look at that ship Katie flew to R&R and it looked a little suspicious to me. Probably some Darkist tech in there, and they can track their stuff."

"So they know where R&R is?" Dare's eyes went wide.

"Possibly, but I doubt they'll attack before we get there."

"Why?"

"Too busy."

"Doing what?"

"Looking for me. Plus Erak can't even go pee without planning every detail."

"Oh. But won't they figure you went back to R&R?"

"No. 'Cause I wouldn't do that. They know that," the redhead grinned. She sat down a barrel and waved at one of the crew members. He started to wave back, before his friend whacked him upside the head.

"So where are we going first? The list you gave the Captain sounded a bit vague." Dare asked.

"That's because these places *are* vague. But I have friends there. So how are you liking your freedom so far?"

"It's uh," Dare frowned at the sudden subject change. "It's good I guess."

"That's good. It's almost 2200, you should get some sleep," Starlight smiled and hopped off her perch. "Good night Dare."

"Night, Starlight."

✪ ✪ ✪

Leaf looked outside his kitchen window and barely raised an eyebrow at the pirate ship anchored in his front yard. Stranger things had happened. He put down his fork and grabbed his backpack on the way to the door. Somehow he wasn't surprised to see his friend Chase standing outside. The redhead grinned and gave him a quick hug. "Leaf! Long time no see!" she laughed. "These are my friends, Dare Ruin and Captain Alastor Azazel. Boys, this is my friend Leaf."

"Why 'ello Chase. I see the details of your death were greatly exaggerated." Leaf grinned, straightening his glasses. "So where are we going this time?"

"Come aboard and yeh'll see." Captain Azazel grinned and looked the young man over. "Lad, yeh do realize that yer hair is pink?"

"Yessir, it is. Is there a problem?" Leaf stared him down.

"Not really, each teh his own then." The Captain shrugged. "Is this it, Trouble?"

"For this dimension? Yep. Let's get going." The redhead grinned.

After locking his door, Leaf followed the three up the ladder to the flying ship. He was greeted with the sight of about fifty pirates and twice as many of Chase's friends.

"Oi! Jordan! Who's the new guy?" One of them called.

"This is Leaf," the redhead replied. "He's awesome."

"Hey Luna, how many more stops?" Someone else asked.

"Two, then we're off," she said.

Dare leaned in and asked, "Starlight, exactly how many names do you have?"

"Too many to count."

"Ah. Where are we going next?"

"Zilos Spaceport to cause some mayhem, then to Earth-235 to pick up a last friend of mine."

"Okay, then what?"

"Then we start the game."

"Game?"

"You'll see," Starlight laughed, a strange glint in her eyes. She took off, leaping into the rigging and swinging away. The ship's engines started and the turbines in the back surged into motion. Dare watched the now familiar sight of setting sail to the sky. Someone had rolled up the ladder and the solar sails were being unfurled. The buzz of the artificial gravity taking hold drowned out all other noises for a few seconds. Then the atmosphere generator sprang to life and the ship was ready to sail.

Beside him, Leaf looked around in approval. "This is most certainly one of the better airships I've seen."

"You've seen a lot?" Dare inquired.

"Yeah. Most everyone in the ΖΣЯΘs either uses airships, or spaceships. Airships being the more *shiplike*. I've seen some crazy looking spaceships but personally, I like airships better. They have a more open plan and in my opinion, are safer."

"Safer?"

"If you hit something or get hit *by* something, an airship stands a better chance than a spaceship. Spaceships are more compact with all the important stuff so they're an easier target. Hit something vital and the craft goes down. On an airship, if the engine or important pieces get hit, the sails will still work, and vice versa. Plus mainly badass guys use airships. Spaceships are for armies, airships are for loners." Leaf continued to drone on for a while more before Dare finally interrupted him, glancing uncomfortably at his watch.

"Yeah, I agree. Hey, I've got to go meet with Starlight and the Captain. See you later." Leaf nodded and moved over to the next unfortunate person.

Dare hurried to the helm where the redhead and Captain Azazel were deep in conversation. Seeing his approach, Starlight grinned, "So… Leaf."

"If I hear the words *spaceship* or *airship* one more time-!" Dare growled.

The other two laughed at his misfortune. "Yeah, Leaf's a talker. Feel free to tell him to shut up at any time. Seriously. Otherwise he'll talk until you're ears fall off." Starlight said.

"Duly noted. How much farther to Zilos?"

"We won't know 'til we use the shortcut drive." Captain Azazel replied. "We need tah get out of this solar system before we can, 'bout ten more minutes."

"Okay, Starlight? Who are we picking up on Earth-whatever it was?"

"A friend of mine…"

"What's their name?"

"Uhh…" the redhead hesitated. "Loki…" she said slowly.

"Loki? As in the one from Asgard? The one that plays tricks on everyone and can't be trusted? That Loki?"

"Yus," she winced. "But he's my friend and he hates the Darkist because they screwed him over way back when. Plus we get along well."

"Of *course* you do. I forgot who I was talking to for a while." Dare's sarcasm was almost tangible.

"Now don't yah be getting on miss Trouble fer her choice in friends, Ruin." The Captain grinned, sending chills down his spine. "Or ye'll be answering teh me. Not that she needs tah be defended."

"Yessir." Dare nodded nervously.

"Lay off, you two!" Starlight shook her head smiling. "Dare, just watch your back. He's harmless really. So unless you're planning to piss him off..."

"No, we're good."

"Good. Alastor, how we doing on the shortcut?"

"Powered up and ready to go."

"Perfect. Let's do this."

❂   ❂   ❂

Joshua looked up from the report he was going over. "Sir. You may want to look at this."

"What? I'm planning. I'll do it later."

"Erak, I think you want to take a look at this," the Commander repeated.

Erak stood up shortly and came over. Glancing over Joshua's shoulder he stared at the report in mounting incredulity. "Whose report is this?"

"Miss DragonSong's. The R&R headquarters have been located, and it seems as if Starlight is gathering forces. She's been appearing all over the ΖΣЯΘs, causing mischief and generally doing what she always does- putting a kink in our plans."

"And?" Erak raised a brow.

"Most of the forces she's getting have personal grudges against us. She's currently in the company of Captain

Azazel. We only know where she has been, no clue as to where she's going."

"Attacking the R&R will bring her running back." Erak mused.

"Not necessarily. She may be on a mission for them. Even if we were to attack, her presence isn't guaranteed. Sir, what exactly are you planning?"

"A plan of attack."

"R&R?"

"Yes, and the last few *free* locations." The General spat.

Joshua mentally groaned. Erak had to plan every little precise detail before he'd even consider presenting the plan to his second in command. Hopefully Starlight would stay away long enough for the supreme leader to at least finish the first phase of his planning. He shook his head and said, "Very well, Sir. I advise you use haste. We have no idea how much time we have. While we wait, our enemies could be planning an attack of their own."

"Commander Flame. I suggest you keep your advice to yourself. You know full well what she's capable of. Every outcome needs to be accounted for."

"Armies have taken down empires with less-"

"So have a few rebels, Commander. So has she." Erak's voice had become dangerously calm. "Do not mistake me for a fool Joshua. I know you want the ZΣЯΘs in our grip, but it takes time. We don't have enough Crystals, nor is our prisoner capable of using them yet. We simply need more time."

"I can give you Time, Sir." Joshua said slowly. "You need only ask."

"Then give me Time." The General's voice was so quiet it could barely be heard, but there was no mistaking the layer of steel in it.

"Yes, Sir."

CHAPTER 16

Joshua was sitting on his bed, staring into space. He was awaiting the arrival of his... acquaintance. The Commander sighed lazily and leaned back, closing his eyes. The room grew dark and shadows seemed to chase each other as a form materialized in the center of the room. The figure was tall, it's skin a dark grey. Black armor covered most of its genderless body. The whites of its eyes seemed to be covered in a red film with the irises entirely black. The red outlines of a Roman numeral clock were glowing on the irises, the hands pointing between the three and four, and a thick ring of golden swirls surrounded the pupil. Its face was surprisingly human and chin length black hair fell from its head, curls framing it's face.

"You called?" Its voice was soft and completely unconcerned.

"Ah, Saniya. I have a task for you." Joshua opened his eyes.

"Yes Master."

"Our General needs a little more Time. What do you suggest?" His voice in comparison was like nails on a blackboard.

The demon grinned. It wasn't often that Joshua asked for its opinion. Perhaps it could get a little amusement out of this job. "I'll think of something. Do you have any requests?"

114

"Just do something about that Starlight girl. She could pose a problem to our plans."

"Of course. How does a little trip through history sound?"

"Perfect. And could you put a Time spell around Erak? He's planning again." Joshua rolled his eyes.

"Of course. Will that be all?"

"Yes," the man sighed. "For now at any rate. You are dismissed."

Saniya bowed and vanished. The shadows disappeared and room returned to its original lighting. "That should keep her occupied." Joshua's smile was made of pure satisfaction.

✪ ✪ ✪

Standing by the open door, Robert sighed. "Jake? You okay?"

"Yeah."

Robert frowned and entered the room. Jake was sitting on a window seat staring out into the sky. "She'll get back soon."

"Yeah."

Shaking his head, Robert smiled sadly. "Jake, you need get up and do something. You can't just sit here on your butt until she comes back."

"You didn't know her, Robby. She would've contacted me if she could. There's something wrong." Jake finally looked at his brother. His face was screwed up in worry and there looked like there was some tear tracks running over his cheeks.

"Jakey, were you crying?" Robert's voice only held concern.

"No! My eyes were just sweating."

"Gross, but okay. Come on. Katie wants us on the bridge. She says she's had an update. You coming?"

"Yeah," Jake wiped his face and nodded. "She's fine." He didn't believe it. There was something wrong. She'd always contact him when she was going to be late. One time her phone died so she hired a group of bikers to swing by the house and sing her message, engines revving along. She always contacted him one way or another. But not this time.

"She's fine," Robert agreed. "Come on." He put an arm around his younger brother's shoulder. Walking through the glossy white hallways to the bridge only took a few seconds and they soon joined their friends.

"Good, everyone's here." Katie said. "Okay. So we have an update on Darkist movement. They're moving their forces into position by Zilos, Lunim, Despine, and R&R."

"R&R? They know where it is?" Ben asked, worried.

The others had mixed reactions. Arya and Lester didn't seem surprised. Katie must have already told them the news. Gil nodded thoughtfully while Scott laughed, "Good, we can wait for them there."

"What about here?" Robert asked.

"It's unknown if they know about this spaceport." Katie admitted. "But the R&R leaders don't want to engage unless provoked. That's the only thing they can agree on. About half want to run, the other half wants to fight. And anyone not with either half are too busy arguing on some other outcome. Arya…" Katie nodded at the princess.

"The rest of us have already agreed that we need to do something about R&R." the elf said. "In order for the R&R to get anything done. I have experience with these kinds of things so we figured that until we can get a more permanent leader, I'd do the job. Robert, since you're officially part of the R&R, you'll be required to report eventually."

"So we're taking over the R&R?" Robert raised his eyebrows.

"We need troops, they need leadership. I'm sure Starlight would agree if she were here."

"But she's not." Jake's voice was low. "And we don't know where she is."

"That's the other part, we received a transmission from the pirate Captain Alastor Azazel." She paused waiting for the sounds of fearful disbelief to fade then continued, "And he says that Starlight and Dare are with him and were planning to meet up with us. Only problem is, she's disappeared."

"Knew it!" Jake said bitterly.

"And the Captain?" Robert pressed.

"He's coming with Dare and Star's... pickups." Katie said. "He didn't say what those pickups were."

"Think we can expect back up?" Scott asked.

"Probably," Gil replied.

"When will they get here?" Ben asked.

"Sometime this week, sooner if they use their shortcut drive." Katie shrugged.

"So what until then?" Lester crossed his arms.

"We plan," Arya said.

❂ ❂ ❂

Previously...

"Okay, you guys stay here, I'll go get Loki." Starlight said. Dare visibly relaxed. "If I'm not back by tomorrow, take everyone to this spaceport. I'll catch up." She handed the Captain the coordinates. "See ya around."

"Be careful miss Trouble," the Captain grinned.

"Bye," Dare said. "Don't die."

"Can't," the redhead grinned and jumped off the ship into the night. She landed on the top of a grassy hill and waved as the ship took off to orbit the planet. This particular Earth seemed to be stuck in the middle ages, with knights and dragons and the whole deal, so flying ships would probably be questioned. *Then again, most Earths would question flying ships,* she grinned. *Now where to find Loki?* She sent a call with her Transporter and was greeted with the sight of a battle.

"Hey, Loki. Oh! Watch out! Geet him! Geet him! Yeah!"

One of the warriors, a golden blonde with twin blades turned around and saw her. "Oh, hello Star-" He dodged a poorly aimed sword stroke. "What are you doing?"

"Looking for you. What are you doing?"

"Fighting what will most likely be known as the Battle of Idiots."

"Lovely. Hey, I've got a proposition for you."

"Do tell." He sliced one of his opponents' head off.

"Well, I'm gathering backup to go against the Darkist." She said. "That one over there is trying to sneak up on you."

"Thanks," Loki threw a dagger at him. "About time."

"Yeah, where are you?"

"Outside Havenport."

"Perfect, I'll meet you there as soon as you're done, yeah?"

"Sounds good to me."

"Okay have fun battling idiots." She grinned and cut the connection. Now to get to Havenport. "Earth-235, Havenport." she intoned and vanished from sight. One of the shadows slithered along the ground to where she was standing and gathered, before vanishing after her.

Starlight reappeared on the outskirts of the town. The sounds of battle could be heard coming from the other side of the town. She grinned and shook her head. Good old death and destruction. She made her way to the local tavern and sat down at a table in the corner to wait. The bartender eyed her warily so she gave him a toothy grin and waved happily. He frowned and went back to cleaning one of the mugs with a dirty rag. She was the only patron in the establishment, everyone else was out fighting or hiding.

The door opened and a suspicious looking fellow wearing a black cloak entered. He waltzed over to her table confidently and sat down across from her. His hood was up and there seemed to be a faint red glow illuminating the inside. He raised his head and stared at her with a smile on his. His eyes were definitely glowing red but they were strange. The irises were tiny clocks complete with tiny hands and an ornamented ring of gold circling the pupils.

She raised her eyebrows and stared back. "Can I help you?"

"No," he- or whatever it was- replied, its voice smooth. "I am simply curious."

"Why?"

"You are a remarkable creature," it said.

"And you're not?"

"Touche. You are immortal."

"So are you, if I'm not mistaken." She leaned back in her chair. "What about it?"

"You have annoyed my Master," It said in a lazy tone. "He wants me to deal with you."

"You are a Time being, correct?"

"Yes. But so are you on occasion, and therein my problem lies." It leaned forward and rested its head on its hands. "My Master wishes you to be sent back in Time, however you could easily just send yourself back. If you do, then I fail my task. I am bound to my Master's bidding. You see how this complicates things. If I cannot carry out my Master's orders then I am forever stuck trying to do something impossible. I would not like to spend my Time as such. Any suggestions?"

The redhead blinked. "How about a bargain?" she proposed. "It sounds to me like your master is also immortal and cannot die, therefore you will never be free. What if I make him mortal and you don't trap me in the past like you obviously plan to, just send me back a good bit?"

"Yes, but you will still send yourself back."

"How about I promise I won't, and in the mean time I'll make this dude mortal. In return you don't trap me. How does that sound? Time really has no meaning for me anyway, so it's not like it'll inconvenience me that much."

"That is a suitable arrangement. Do you swear it?"

"Just how far back would you be sending me?"

"Far enough. How would you like to be with your family again?" Its smile was eerie.

"That's pretty far back. I'd have a lot of time to do exactly what your master doesn't want me doing." She pointed out.

"That is true, but I'm also sure he wouldn't want you turning him mortal either."

"Point. Before I forget, who *is* your master?"

"You are a smart being. Most people would have forgotten to ask that."

"Yeah well, I'm probably forgetting a lot of other things, so just humor me. The harder you make it for me, the harder you make it for yourself."

"Joshua Flame."

"Really? Figures," she grumbled. "Okay you have yourself a deal. I'll set you free and won't try to send myself back here so long as you don't trap me in Time." She held out her hand.

"I won't trap you in Time so long as you set me free and don't try to return." He extended his hand.

"This will probably take a while. No time limits."

"No time limits," It agreed and they shook on it. Immediately its eyes started to glow gold and the tiny hands on the clocks in his eyes started spinning. Then there was a flash she was gone. The bartender looked up and glared, completely unconcerned that someone had just vanished into thin air from his tavern. The hooded figure nodded at him, stood, and left the establishment.

CHAPTER 17

Even previously-er...

Starlight looked around. She was sitting in a very different tavern from the one she started out in. This one was full of patrons and the noise level was high. She was still in a corner, but that did nothing to ease her discomfort. Immediately she changed her appearance, her trademark vibrant red hair and green eyes being replaced by a light brown and blue. The place was well lit and the smells of food, ale, and smoke permeated the air. No one seemed to notice her sudden arrival but then again the place was pretty crowded to begin with. Someone had started a song and many had joined in at the chorus.

She sat watched wondering where and *when* exactly she was. Hopefully sometime close to when she wanted to be. The song was a familiar one and the friendly atmosphere soon put her nerves at rest. So much so that she found herself joining in at the next chorus. She could spend the night here then find out the information she was missing tomorrow. Surely one night wouldn't matter.

She ordered a meal and was soon joined by some of the others. Soon deep in conversation, Starlight was smiling and laughing along with the rest of her new acquaintances. One man was telling a particularly amusing story about a cat he had found when she spotted her man. A significantly younger looking Joshua sat down next to a dark haired man at one of the wall tables on the opposite side of the room. They exchange a few words and had a round of drinks before getting up and exiting the establishment.

She wasted no time, saying goodbye to her companions and making her way out the door. She looked around and finding no one looking at her, she faded out of the visible spectrum. Joshua and his buddy were walking up the street towards the town gates. This town was slightly less primitive than the one before, but was still mostly made of wood. Where the other town was surrounded by plains, this one was on the edge of a forest. A forest that the two men were heading for.

She followed silently behind them. They took a path through the trees until they came to a small clearing with a round thatched hut in the center. Smoke was rising from a hole in the middle of the roof and the whole place looked like it belonged to some kind of witch doctor.

Bones and odd things that did who knows what were hanging all over. Starlight watched as the men entered the hut. Unsure as to whether her presence would be noticed, she crept forwards and peered into a window on the side of the hut. The conversation going on inside was very informative.

"You said it would work." Joshua was saying.

"You did not complete the instructions." Starlight couldn't tell if the ancient voice belonged to a man or a woman. The individual so thin she almost mistook the resident as one of the skeletons hanging around the place.

"Yes I did. It didn't work." Joshua insisted.

"Then you did not do it correctly."

"But I did! I followed your instructions to the letter, nothing happened!"

"Did I not say that it would take a few days for the effects to be noticeable?" The old man- Starlight thought it was a man- croaked. "Be patient."

"I want the rest of it." Joshua demanded.

"If the effects are not apparent then it is too soon."

"It's been a month!" he burst out angrily. "You said it would take two or three weeks!"

"Obviously for you it takes longer. I said on average!" the wiry man snapped.

"Give me the rest of it old man!"

"You will not like the results. You need to wait longer for it to work properly."

"I don't care. I need it now!"

"Very well. Don't say I didn't warn your sorry carcass," the old man grumbled. He grabbed a bottle off one of his shelves. Inside was a glowing blue potion, the same color as the Portal Crystal... Stone- things. "Drink this, then go away. I don't want to see you here again. Let me know in the next life how immortality works for you. Oh wait, that's right you *won't be able to die.*"

Joshua eagerly snatched the bottle and wasted no time chugging the liquid down. He ignored the man's quips and glanced at his companion. "Let's go." They left and Starlight was very tempted to follow them but then the old man addressed her.

"You can come in you know. I know you're there."

She winced and reappeared into view on her way to the door. No way was she climbing in through his creepy bone filled window. Entering the hut, she grinned sheepishly and rubbed the back of her neck. "I guess there's no point in asking how you knew I was there?"

The man smiled and gestured to a chair. They both sat down and he got straight to the point. "You were following them?"

"Yes. I'm trying to stop him from becoming immortal or find a way to undo it."

"Ah, then take this. Spray it in his face within the next hour and you may undo the spell." He handed her what looked like an improvised aerosol can.

"What is it?"

"Pepper spray." He laughed.

"And that's going to do… what exactly?"

"I'd like to see the look on his face when you do."

"Really? *Really?* Dude! I need something better than that! Come on, my productive life kinda depends on it!"

"I'm sorry. The only offer I can give you is this: In exactly five thousand years, he will have a choice to give up his immortality or keep it. My advice: Make his existence hell. Hopefully he'll do anything to be mortal again. He took the potion too soon. He may be unable to die, but he can still get hurt. He can still catch illness, he just can't *die.*"

"Okay… I can work with this. And what Time am I in?"

"About five thousand years before your original Time."

"I'll take your word for it…"

"Telmarkin."

"Well Telmarkin, it was nice meeting you. I'm Starlight. Anything else I need to know before I leave?" the redhead asked.

"Yes. When his choice comes, make sure you don't stand in the line of fire." Telmarkin advised.

"Wait what?"

"It will all make sense eventually," he snapped. "Now go away, I have work to do!"

"Alright then." She shook her head and walked out. "Great… five thousand years. Might as well make the most of it. I wonder where the past me is right now."

✪ ✪ ✪

The sun was just rising as Joshua entered the Hall of Portals. Even at the early hour, the place was filled with traffic. Most of the occupants on Planet Four were still asleep, but the Hall was always open. Serving as an in between place, the Hall allowed people from all over the ZΣЯΘs to travel anywhere there was a Portal. Most of the benches were occupied, but he managed to claim an empty one down one of the less used hallways.

The main room was still in sight, but only a few travelers were passing through here. The man took the opportunity to glance around suspiciously. Ever since he had left that stupid old man's house he had been plagued by some unseen force. It laughed at him when he tripped. After warning him against doing something, it enjoyed his cries of pain filled annoyance when he proceeded to do it anyway. He couldn't sleep at night due to its insistent repetition of 'poke, poke, poke,' while carrying out the action. This thing was slowly driving him insane!

Just as he had started to relax, it made its presence known by shoving him off the bench and onto the floor. The passersby mostly gave him strange looks while some laughed. A ghostly laugh echoed around him, its gleeful tone mocking him. Joshua angrily picked himself up and grabbed his bag: He wouldn't be getting any rest here.

The unfortunate immortal was too busy fuming to look where he was going and collided with a young woman with tousled white hair and a pair of light blue glasses framing her green eyes. She looked to be in quite a hurry and was very put out at having to collect her bags; one of which had burst open, spilling its contents all over the floor.

"Hey! Watch it!" she snapped angrily adjusting her glasses, which had been knocked askew.

"Sorry. I-" Joshua froze at the sight before him. Two of the girl's things were floating towards her bag, as if held by someone. Then two more. His tormentor was helping her pick up! Taking advantage of its distraction, the immortal took off without so much as a glance at the poor girl.

The girl glared after him then glanced behind her and found a brown haired young woman returning her belonging to their bag. She bent down to help muttering apologies.

"Don't worry about it. He's a jerk. I'm Gianna," the woman smiled.

"Seron. And thank you. Where are you headed?" she brushed her white hair out of her face.

"Returning home to Four actually." Gianna said as Seron zipped up her bag.

"Really? I'm here visiting- or well looking for a job really." Seron grinned.

"You have somewhere to stay?" Gianna asked.

"Uh…"

"Don't worry, I've got an extra room." Gianna said decidedly. "So where ya coming from?"

"The Hama region. But I couldn't keep up with the taxes so I got evicted. Came here to start fresh." The two girls made their way to the exit and walked out into the open.

Back in the Hall, Starlight had a decision to make. *Follow Joshua, or my younger self and new friend Seron?* she thought. *Joshua will still be here for a good long while and I can always check up on him…* She nodded, decision made and followed the girls outside.

CHAPTER 18

Seron was most certainly an interesting character. Almost as interesting as a Blender when it came down to it. Gianna had taken her home and given her the guest room in her small apartment. The moment she was alone, she took off her glasses and rubbed the bridge of her nose. Several things happened.

Her skin turned an icy blue, the same color as her glasses, while the glasses themselves turned white. A pair of majestic white and light green feathered wings appeared on her back, and her left eye turned a cloudy dead white color. She sighed and sat down on the bed, spreading her wings out and flopping down so she was lying down.

Starlight watched all this in amusement, still invisible before wondering how long before her younger self found out about it. It didn't matter really. She had no memory of this, so it hadn't happened the last time. Joshua probably hadn't knocked her over so Gianna had never met her.

Starlight grinned, time to go confuse the heck out of said younger self. She phased through the thin walls and found Gianna in the kitchen. The older version sat herself down at the small table and became visible again, watching Gianna cook dinner.

The brunette turned around and saw Starlight sitting there, uninvited and certainly unexpected. She didn't even bat an eye. "Hi, how can I help you?"

"It's Star," the redhead grinned.

"Perfect, past or future?" Gianna shot back and a rapid fire conversation started.

"Future."

"Anything interesting happen?"

"Yeah, lots, but I won't spoil it for you. You know Erak Darke?"

"What about him?"

"Well, I figured out how he never gets any older, and seems to pop up all the time."

"Really?"

"Yeah, his number two has a Time Demon."

"Ah, makes sense, he is human after all."

"Right, but the thing is, that's going to be a problem. Joshua, Mr. Number Two, has it messing up our stuff, and it will eventually allow them to win. And I also kinda sorta possibly made a deal with it."

"Figures."

"Yeah, so now I have to make Joshua a mortal again so it doesn't have to listen to him or it will trap me in some kind of time loop and I'll be out of the picture."

"Well, we can't have that."

"No, but now I have like about five thousand years to do extra sneaky things."

"Need any help?"

"Yeah hang tight and annoy the Darkist."

"Will do."

"So that new friend of yours…"

"What about her?"

"She's cool." Starlight grinned. Then the bedroom door opened and Seron walked in.

"Hey Gianna, who's this?" she asked.

"I'm her sister, Starlight. Just here visiting. I've got to go soon, just thought I'd check up on little sis here."

"Nice to meet you."

"Likewise. Well, I'll see you around kids." The red head bowed and headed out the door. "Stuff to see and people to do and all that."

Seron and Gianna looked at each other, then burst out laughing. "That's your sister?" Gianna wiped the tears from her eyes.

"Yup, good old Star. Predictably unpredictable."

"Nice. I wish I had a sister."

"Don't we all."

✪ ✪ ✪

The Crossroads, as she had taken to calling it, was the same as she had left it. Up ahead the city still gave of a bright white light and to her left the mist was still as thick as ever. She had a plan to implement, but first she had some exploring to do. She glanced down the right hand path towards the mountains. The red glow gave her the heebeegeebees. Examining the mountains in more detail this time, she noticed that they looked to be made out of hardened lava that had been cracked and pushed up by multiple earthquakes.

The dirt path wound down the slope, badly cut stairs with bits of twisted metal imbedded in the dry earth outlining the route, to a hole in the bottom of the nearest mountain. Standing at the edge of the Crossroads, Starlight could feel the heat radiating from that hole. All was silent, and she reached out with her Soul Force to test the atmosphere. Recoiling almost instantly, she gaped at the hole. Each wave of heat brought forth a feeling of agony and despair.

Steeling herself against the onslaught, the redhead forced her feet to travel down the stairs descending towards the hole. She put up mental shield after mental shield to keep the horrors out and continued until she reached the edge of the hole, which turned out to be a gap in the ceiling of what she could only describe as hell. If the city was Heaven than this most certainly was Hell.

The edge she was standing on dropped down into a cliff beneath her feet, the wall plunging straight down and made of dark rock. At the bottom, the ground was littered with large sharp rocks and sloped slowly down to the shores of a lake. As far as she could tell, the lake was either made out of lava or liquid fire. Wisps of steam were rising off the surface and gathering in a cloud on the ceiling. Small waves washed up along the rocky beach, and a pier extended out over the lake. At the end was a circular piece with benches on either side.

It was too far away to see the details, but Starlight could see tiny round things bobbing in the fire. Everything but the waves was deadly still. Red haze surrounded the area and she couldn't see the far side of the lake, but the redhead felt sure that the cavern extended on far past the fiery waves.

Most certainly not reassured by the area's silence, Starlight leaned farther over the edge to see if there was a way down. The cliff face was smooth and there were no paths leading down. Apparently one was expected to jump. Not a problem if you had wings however.

"When in Rome..." she muttered, adding with a smirk, "Do as the *Romanians* do." An impressive pair of red bat-like wings sprouted on her back as she jumped into the hole. There must have been some kind of invisible barrier over the opening, because she was immediately greeted with strong turbulence pushing her towards the cliff. She flailed around for a few seconds before regaining her balance with a determined flap of her wings and descended to the ground. She landed on her feet with her knees bent and looked around.

There were hundreds of small caves littering the lower half of the cliff that she hadn't been able to see before. Down here, below the dangerous winds by the ceiling, the silence was broken by various noises. The caves were filled with creatures, all currently out of sight, and there were splashes coming from the lake. A few of the round things seemed to be flailing around, arms extended.

A harmonious hissing suddenly came from the caves that turned into warnings. *"Demons coming, run, hide."*

Starlight's head whipped around at the sound of harsh voices coming from her right, behind some of the larger rocks on the beach. "An intruder?" one growled. "Who would be fool enough to intrude here?"

"It's happened before," the other voice said.

"Yeah well they were stupid, caught soon enough. Handed over to the Others. Why do we need to guard this area? No one can climb up the cliff, and that shield stops people from getting out anyhow."

Starlight gulped and glanced at the caves. The hissing had gone silent. Even if their occupants were afraid of Demons, that didn't mean they wouldn't attack her. The sounds of the two guards were drawing closer. She made a snap decision and bolted for the nearest cave.

It was one of the smaller caves and as she backed away from the entrance she began to hear a fast ticking sound. The closer she got, the faster it got. She turned around and blinked, changing to night vision. Glancing around, she found that the source of the ticking was a small quivering shape huddled by the back of the cave. It was shaped like an egg and *looking* at her. As she stepped closer it tried to burrow itself into the wall in an attempt to hide.

"Hey," she whispered. "Hey, it's ok little guy. I'm not going to hurt you." She crouched down to its level and smiled reassuringly. "What's a little guy like you doing down here?"

The thing ticked at her, blinked, and a pair of arms appeared from behind it and wrapped around itself. If it had had knees, then it would be hugging them tight. Starlight continued to talk to it, and eventually it began to relax. "You're not so bad after all, are you, little guy?" she grinned as it inched forwards, a nervous look on its adorable little face. Then there was a sound from outside and it dived back to its place by the back wall.

"Check the caves he says. They could be hiding he says. There's nothing here but monsters that will eat them!" one of the Demons was right outside.

Starlight panicked and turned invisible, causing the little guy behind her to start ticking faster again. The Demon looked inside and saw it huddled in the back. "Hey! There you are! We've been looking all over for you! Get over here Tokemi! Boss wants you back."

Tokemi shook and ticked so hard that the Demon rolled his eyes and started to grab him. Then Starlight stepped in and threw up a hand, blasting ice at the creepy thing. It was frozen in place, but she didn't know for how long as it was pretty warm down here.

Tokemi looked at her in awe and perked up, coming to life. His arms were made of circular clocks, now that she had a closer look, and he had little horns on top of his head that curved outwards. On his belly he had another clock that was spinning as if it couldn't tell what time it was. He was hovering about a foot off the ground on three light blue circles getting smaller as they neared the ground, which brought his overall height to about three feet.

He smiled at her and ticked affectionately, snuggling up to her legs and butting his head against her hand. She giggled and petted him then knelt and said, "Tokemi- that is you name right?" He smiled and tickled. "Okay, Tokemi, we need to get out of here, I don't know if you know what I'm saying so tick once for no and twice for yes."

Tick tick.

"Good, okay then, do you know a way out of here?"

Tick tick.

"Okay, can you get me out of here?"

Tick tick.

"Okay then, let's go."

Tick tick. He smiled and started bouncing out of the cave. He peered out and checked that there was no one around, then bounced out into the open with Starlight right behind him. He looked at her wings then at the lake and repeated the action. "You want me to fly over the lake?"

Tick tick.

"I don't know if I can, it's pretty hot by the fire and there are strong winds up near the ceiling. Is there a way around on the shore?"

Tokemi hesitated then ticked twice and started shaking violently.

"Yes, but it's dangerous."

Tick tick.

"Right then, but if I can't fly right and we fall into the fire, we're done for. And isn't the way out up there not on the other side of the lake?"

Tick, tick tick.

"Yes and no? Do we need to go get something from the other side of the lake to get out?"

Tick tick!

"Okay, you wanna try flying?" Tokemi looked at her and ticked very fast creating a purring noise. "You'll do whatever I do?" she guessed.

Tick tick.

"Okay then, let's try the beach, there's plenty of rocks to hide behind right?"

Tick tick, he seemed to sigh and took off along the beach with his new protector right behind him.

❂ ❂ ❂

Joshua hid his growing insanity very well. He could still focus on his work, though it was hard and very sloppy. He thought eventually that he'd just fall asleep from exhaustion, but apparently not. That infernal *thing* just wouldn't let him sleep! It would sabotage his plans, embarrass him in front of his superiors and what few friends he still had left, and no one else seemed to hear the constant obnoxious laughter.

He felt himself nodding off and right on cue the poltergeist started its work poking him in all sorts of places and saying 'poke' with each one. "Poke, poke, poke, poke, poke."

"I'm awake!" he yelled desperately. When he had first heard the voice he had just thought he was hearing things but now after centuries of its talking he had started to believe what it said. *Your choice is coming up soon. You can be mortal again. You can* die. *Wouldn't that be better than this terrible existence?*

Yes, he thought. *Oh hell yes!* But he had never said it out loud. The old man had warned him that he would regret taking the potion too early, and to admit he wanted it to stop would be to let the old man win. He would *not* let the old man win. He *would not!*

"I'm awake," he repeated. "Please can I just sleep for a minute? I can't *do* anything." He would not let the old man win, but he was not above pleading with the thing.

"You can sleep when you have made your choice," it whispered. "Not before. The old man warned you remember?"

"Yes, yes! When is the choice?"

"Soon," it said. *Soon.* It always said that.

"How soon?"

"Very soon. Keep working, you don't want Erak to get mad at you."

"Screw Erak. I'm tired."

"Poke…"

"I'm working! I'm working!"

CHAPTER 19

Starlight and Tokemi hid behind one of the rocks for the umpteenth time. Tokemi was right, the beach was practically crawling with nasties. They were about halfway through and had almost been spotted too many times. Still unsure as to where they were going, Starlight followed the little Demon through the maze of rocks.

After what seemed like hours, they finally reached the edge of the rocks. "What now?" Starlight whispered.

Tokemi pointed towards the ever present swirling red haze. It was just clear enough to make out some kind of twisted structure. "We're going there?!"

Tick tick.

"Just great. Why do we need to go there? Isn't that where you were escaping from?"

Tick tick.

"Then did you forget something?"

Tick tick.

"Is it really that important?"

Tick tick! Tick tick!

"Okay okay! We'll go get it. Do you know where you left it?"

Tick tick, he pointed to the highest spire.

"That's just peachy. Okay, can we fly up there? Is there like a window or something?"

Tick tick. Tick tick tick tick tick.

"Yes, but there's trouble?" She had figured out he would tick five times to warn her of danger. "Okay, like what kind of danger? Like we'll be see- Oh. That kind of trouble." Flying around the... Castle, for lack of a better term, was a huge, spiky, fire breathing *dragon*. Her eyes got wide- that could also ignite itself on fire. "Perfect."

Tick tick tick. Let's go. He urged her on towards the door.

"Wait! We need a plan! What does this thing look like?"

Tokemi pointed towards the clocks on his arms, then pointed towards one of the ones closer to his three fingered hand. It was missing. There was just an empty circle. "Oh you left your clock behind!"

Tick tick! Tick tick!

"Okay, well stay here. I can get in and out faster that way."

Tick!

"Tokemi please. You need that clock, and I need to get out of here. Just humor me. Hide behind the rock and stay put. I know you want to come, but you can't turn invisible like I can, or fly, or teleport, or- well you get the picture."

The little Demon sighed and pointed to his clocks. *Tick tick tick!* They all began spinning and he started to glow. Then it all stopped as soon as it started and he frowned, pointing to the empty circle.

"Wait..." Starlight said slowly, an epiphany on its way. "You can control Time? You're a Time demon?"

Tick tick! he grinned proudly.

"But you can't get out because one of your clocks are missing."

Tick tick.

"Okay, stay here. I'll go get it. I'll be back in... There's no Time here is there? Well, I'll be back... soon then."

Tick. But he seemed to sit down and accept the decision. Starlight nodded and faded from sight, taking off into the air.

She could take on the dragon, after all there was only the one while there were who knows how many nasties inside the castle. Riding the gusts slowly and carefully, she timed the passage of the dragon so she'd hit the window while it was on the other side. Reaching the window, she gripped the edge and looked in. There was no one in sight so she slipped gracefully inside and ducked just as the dragon came around again. Luckily the winds had carried her scent away.

The room was circular with grotesque twisting pillars making up the walls. It looked like some sort of treasury with piles of stuff everywhere and locked chests scattered around. She sent out a Soulforce probe: If it was part of Tokemi then it should register with her internal reader. It was locked in one of the chests on the far side. She hurried over and tried opening the lock. Nothing. She looked around and saw tons keys hanging by the door. *It's gotta be one of those,* she thought and darted over.

Scanning the keys, she saw one in particular that caught her eye. *Is this what I think this is?* Pulling it carefully from its hook, she examined its plain exterior. She took it over to the nearest chest and fitted into the lock. It opened. The chest sprung open and she found it was filled with clothes of all things. All black one piece suits. She grabbed one for further examination and headed back to the chest containing Tokemi's clock. That chest opened as well.

Who just leaves a Skeleton Key lying around like that? she wondered and grabbed the clock. It was heavier than she expected. After the initial shock, Starlight hefted it up and make her way back to the window. The dragon continued to fly circles around the spire and as soon as it has passed she jumped out with suit and clock in hand.

As soon as the items had left the room an alarm went off. The dragon came to a stop and hovered, furiously looking around for the intruder. The window was heavy with her scent and after getting a whiff of her, it soared after her. Starlight hastily landed by Tokemi and handed him the clock. He grinned with joy once it was in his hands and put it back in its place.

"Okay little guy, now we need to go. Like right now. Which is safer, the beach or flying?"

The little Demon flapped his arms. "Flying, okay good. Let's go." She grabbed him and took off into the sweltering air. The Dragon had traced her progress and was flying after them, searching for her invisible form. She flapped with all her might, sending them racing through the air over the lake. The winds were starting to take effect and she slowed considerably, but so did the dragon. Hordes of Demons and other nasties had joined the chase, both along the beach and in the air.

Starlight rolled her eyes at her progress and changed tactics. Angling her body for a straight shot back to the Hole, she raised her wings to a gliding position and blasted fire out of the soles of her feet. The two were instantly jettisoned at a tremendous speed towards their exit, outstripping their pursuers. She took a chance and blasted right through the shield covering the Hole. She stopped the flame once they were out and landed on the stairs to the Crossroads.

Unfortunately her shoes and the bottoms of her pants had been incinerated in the maneuver and she had landed right on top of one of the metal shards that littered the place. Clutching her foot, she cursed and sat down hard, eyes trained on the entrance to the Hole. The nasties couldn't seem to break through the shield so she congratulated herself.

"Job well done! Now we know that they won't be a problem and my construction will be perfectly safe." She high fived Tokemi, who seemed to love the gesture and repeated it several times.

Tick tick! Tick tick! Tick tick! Tokemi smiled.

"Come on cutie, wanna see what I'm making?" she healed her foot and picked up the suit heading up the stairs.

Tick tick!

✪ ✪ ✪

Joshua moaned. The thing still wouldn't leave him alone. It had been over three thousand years and he hadn't gotten a wink of sleep. At this point he just wanted to go to sleep and *never* wake up. Erak was getting more annoying and the constant presence of his tormenter wasn't doing him any favors. He had told Erak about it once, and the General had chalked it up to his personal nemesis, Star. But Joshua had seen Star plenty of times and if anything, her presence seemed to deter the poltergeist.

No, it wasn't her. Something else was giving him his own personal hell. "How soon until my choice?" he whispered.

"Soon."

"How soon?" He begged desperately.

"Soon enough."

Joshua put his head down so it wouldn't see the angry tears that escaped his eyes. "I'm not sleeping!" he said. "Just leave me alone! ... Please."

Loki tilted his head. The guy was crying. The dude was actually crying! Starlight was right, it was almost too easy.

✪ ✪ ✪

Starlight looked around at the area. Situated on a slight hill, it was the perfect place to build her construction. Tokemi seemed to like it so she nodded to herself and began her work. Portal Crystals were actually used for some other things than making Transports, although she'd be making plenty of those too. The first thing to go up had been the Forcefield around the path. She didn't want anyone going off the path.

"Tokemi, come here!" she called.

The little Demon scurried over to meet her. *Tick tick?*

"You wanted to help right?"

Tick tick!

"Okay then, we are going to build a new home."

Tick tick?

"Yup, and lots of people are going to live here."

Tick tick!

"Let's get to work then!"

CHAPTER 20

Starlight glanced up at the clock on Main Street. Less than thirty five years until she caught up with her original Time. *I need something to do until then.* She looked around the square and saw a class of Fives taking a tour of the city. She grinned, seeing one redhead in particular. *Rose Fyler. Perfect.* She ducked into an alley and adjusted her appearance accordingly. No one noticed when a young blonde haired child joined the group.

Rose was near the back of the group and Starlight fell into step beside her. "Hi." her voice was high and clear. "I'm Luna. What's your name?"

"Rose." The redhead looked surprised to see another child there, as if no one usually talked to her. "You're not in my class."

"Not before, but I am now. I just moved here. I'm starting school tomorrow and mama said I should make some friends."

"I'll be your friend." Rose said seriously. "But I have to warn you. Most people don't like me."

"Well, *I* like you." Starlight grinned. "I also like your hair. Red hair is my favorite!"

"Come on Luna!" Rose shouted. "Hurry up!"

"But the water is cold!" Starlight complained. The two best friends were on a summer camping trip with Rose's family and were staying near some waterfalls.

"It's a river! Of course it's cold! Are you coming in or what?"

"It's too cold!" Starlight insisted shuffling her feet on the rock platform by the bank of the rapids. Downstream the small waterfalls made a rushing sound.

"Oh come *on*! It's not *that* cold!" Rose groaned. Tomorrow was her twelfth birthday and she certainly wasn't going to let it start with her best friend *not* going in the water.

Back at the cabin Rose's parents were sitting on the porch watching the girls. "Stefin, don't you find it odd that we've never met Luna's parents?" Rose's mom asked.

"Well, they *do* work a lot Amber."

"Yes, but we've *never* seen them. They've never come over. They're never home when we stop by and they never come to parent night at the girl's school."

"They're just busy, dear. Rosie sees them when she stays the night. Luna's mother baked that pie last week for Rosie's party. You've talked to them on the phone and there are plenty of pictures-" Stefin shrugged.

"Yes, but have you ever actually *seen* either of them?" Amber insisted.

"No. But-"

"Exactly. Isn't it strange that we've never met them and the girls have been best friends for years?"

"I suppose. Perhaps we should invite them over?" Stefin suggested.

"I doubt they'll come. Too busy as usual. Where do they work anyway?" Amber frowned.

"Luna said her father is usually away on business trips and her mother is a government agent."

"So you're telling me that they're usually never home? They just leave her by herself? She's just a child, how's she supposed to take care of herself?"

"She has that strange pet of hers that follows her around everywhere, and that robot-"

"A robomaid and a pet?" Amber asked in disgust. "It's a wonder she can function, let alone how polite she is. Ask her how often her parents are home. There are laws about child neglect you know."

"Amber, does she look neglected to you?" Stefin gestured to the two laughing girls. Rose has succeeded in pulling Luna into the water and the blonde haired girl was shrieking and splashing with a vengeance. She certainly didn't look neglected.

"She's at our house most of the time, Stefin. She sleeps in Rosie's room more than she sees the inside of her own home. She's practically Rosie's sister," Amber said.

"So? Amber, honey, it's not our job to criticize her parents. She's a perfectly happy, normal child, with nice loving parents. She's fine."

Amber sighed and shook her head. "I just think it's strange that's all. I'm going to arrange a meeting with them."

"Alright dear, if it will make you happy."

"Yes."

Tokemi scuttled out from his perch under the porch and hurried to the girls ticking furiously. He bounced up and down on the platform to get their attention. "Woah! What is it boy?" Rose asked. "What's wrong?"

Starlight swam over and grabbed the edge of the rock platform. "Hey Tokemi. It's okay, what's wrong?"

Tick tick tick tick tick.

"Trouble? What's trouble?" The little Demon pointed at the house. "The house?"

Tick.

"Rosie's parents?"

Tick tick!

"What about my parents?" Rose asked. Tokemi pointed at Starlight, then at Rose's parents again.

"My parents?" Starlight asked, catching on.

Tick tick!

"They want to see my parents?"

Tick tick!

The girls looked at each other and gulped. "Well... they were going to ask eventually." Starlight winced.

"Yeah, but you don't have any parents." Rose said.

"I know. Holograms wouldn't work because they'd want to shake hands."

"What about having someone else stand in? Maybe your Illusionator friends?" Rose suggested.

"All busy..."

"You could pretend to be them...?"

"I'd only be able to be one at a time, and they expect me to be there too."

"Can't you do that mind thing on them?"

"No, that only works for suggestions, like talking to the police. Not altering what people see."

"What about Robby? Wasn't he working on some kind of semi solid holograms?"

"The holo-me's? Those could work, but we'd need to program them on what to say, where to walk, what to do... there's just too many possibilities." Starlight shot down the idea.

"But what about your... alters?"

Starlight's eyes darted around in thought. "That... could... work..."

"Then let's call him!" Rose grinned.

"Okay, but you do it!"

"What, why?"

"Cause it was your idea!"

"But-"

"No buts! You call him and we'll both talk."

"Okay fine!" Rose pouted. The two girls gathered on the platform and huddled together. Starlight got her Transporter ready and held it out as Rose grabbed hold. It turned out that if more than one person had a hold of it when you started a call then you could both be seen on the other end.

"Message, Kapital City, Planet Four, Isis dimension, Robert Gilgalad."

The two waited as a screen appeared in front of them, linking to his computer. Robert's face appeared and grinned. "Hey girls! Whacha doing?" He was significantly younger than the man Starlight had seen during the escape plan but the resemblance was there.

"Hi Robby!" Rose smiled.

"Hi Robby!" Starlight grinned, elbowing her friend in the ribs.

"Okay okay! Uh, we have a question for you," Rose said.

"Alright shoot." The fifteen year old genius laughed.

"You know those holograms you were working on?"

"The Holo-me's?"

"Yeah," Rose blushed. "Those things. Have you finished them?"

"Just working out the kinks. I'm working on a supercomputer that's smart enough to make them act on their own with a few prompts, but for now you still have to program them," Robert shrugged. "Why, you wanna try them out?"

"My parents want to meet Luna's," Rose said. "But..."

"She doesn't have any, right. Well, they're going to ask questions so you'll need to plan for that and-"

"We've got it covered. You know that thing you were thinking of making, the machine that connects your mind to a computer?" Starlight asked.

"Yeah, I was thinking of using it for a virtual reality thing."

"Yeah that. So have you made it yet?"

"I started it, but I got side tracked."

"Then you need to get back on it!" Starlight declared. "How long do you need to finish it?"

"I don't know, a week?"

"Okay, so we'll plan the Operation Meet the Parents for next Thursday then? Will that be enough time?"

"That should just about do it." Robert said. "I'll get to work now."

"Great see you Wednesday?"

"Yup."

"Bye Robby!" Rose and Starlight chorused.

"Bye girls."

The link terminated as Robby hung up. The girls looked at each other and grinned. They would drop the news to Rose's parents at dinner. Hopefully they would be satisfied.

Wednesday dawned bright and early and the girls hurried over to Robert's house. Jake answered the door, "Hey girls. Robby said you'd be over today. You guys are working on some super-secret project?"

"Yeah, my parents want to meet Luna's." Rose explained.

"Ah, well come on in. You know you don't really have to knock." Jake grinned.

"We were just being polite." Starlight smirked.

"You polite?" he scoffed. "Right."

Starlight smiled nostalgically. Jake was the same as she remembered, annoying and loved you to death. It was ironic really, she knew him as a twelve year old kid and loved him like a brother. Back in her own time the same was true. Some things just never changed.

The three walked down the stairs to Robert's basement workshop and met him by the door. "Alright Robby, whacha got?" Starlight asked.

"Ok, so I finished the thing you wanted, and I touched up the Holo-me's so all the bugs are gone. We just have to upload your consciousness to them and link it to the Holo-me's and we're good to go."

"Okay and how long is that going to take?" Rose asked. "Cause I have to be back for dinner."

"I don't know." Robert shrugged. "So we'll just have to wait and see."

"I've got a question," Starlight said. "So about the uploading thing, does it have to be my entire mind or just parts of it?"

"Depends, how complicated is your mind?"

"Very."

"Then only parts, this would help if you could make some sort of-"

"I'm using my alters."

"What?"

"My alternate personalities. I've got multiple personality disorder, remember?"

"Oh yeah, on account of you being so old. It's kinda hard to remember, you've got a pretty good handle on them."

"Yeah about that," Jake said. "When are you going to tell us everything? We know you can change your appearance more than the average person, you're actually old as dirt, and you know things you shouldn't."

"I told you," Starlight said. "I'll tell you when it's the right Time."

"So you keep saying." Jake shook his head. "Alright, let's get this party started!"

They hooked Starlight up to a machine that looked like it was made of stuff from an old man's garage, attaching electrodes to her temples while she got comfy on the couch. Believe it or not, it was the same couch from the future Robert's Darkist lab/cell. He must have gotten most of his old stuff in there.

"This isn't going to hurt, is it?" Starlight asked, resigned to the worst.

"Um... Probably not, or at least it shouldn't if my calculations are right," Robert mumbled, making sure everything was working properly.

"Okay, good." Starlight wasn't sure if she believed him.

"Okay, here we go," Robert said and turned it on.

Starlight closed her eyes and waited, but nothing happened. After a while she opened her eyes and immediately changed that assumption.

CHAPTER 21

She opened her eyes and stopped dead. She was sitting on the bed of her old room. Her original old room in Atlantis. She hadn't see it since the Move. Scattered around the room were various people. They all had red hair and green eyes like her favorite appearance, but they were dressed very differently.

In all her time, she had never actually seen what her alters looked like. She just knew there were a lot and that they sometimes surfaced when she hit her head really hard. She'd usually use some of their names to help with her disguises, taking on certain traits but she was just guessing there. Here and now she could literally tell them apart by the way they were dressed. All were dressed in shades of green, brown, and black, they all had some kind of blue gem on them somewhere, and they all had the same face as Starlight, but that's where the similarities stopped.

She sat on the bed awkwardly until one of them spoke up. "Hi, you're Starlight."

"Yes..." Starlight confirmed slowly.

"I'm Trouble!" She was wearing a green short sleeved shirt with a light brown open jean vest on top with brown skinny jeans on her legs. Her hair was messy and up in a ponytail. She had bandages on her face, elbows, and knees and was wearing a necklace that looked exactly like her

150

Transporter. "This is Chase, Anna, Luna, Mari, Ivy, Jordan, and Simon."

Chase spoke up next with a grin, "It's nice to finally meet you, Star. Trouble here was the first alter to appear, then me, Anna, and Luna showed up pretty close together. After that came Simon, Mari, and Jordan. And finally Ivy." She had short hair that was longer at the top and spiked up. She was wearing a sleeveless top with a collar that came up her neck a bit and dark green edging along it and down the zipper. Over that she had on a black leather jacket, black cargo pants, and the same Transporter. Topping off the look was a pair of aviator glasses, a mic and earpiece, some ear piercings, a scar on her right cheek, and a sword at her back. She would most likely get along with Dare just fine.

The only way to describe Anna was to say she looked like a regular college student. Her hair was up in a braided updo with the ends free. She had on a green collared shirt open at the throat with a brown leather jacket on top and blue jeans on her lower half. A pair of black glasses perched on her nose and from one of her ears hung a blue gem, most likely her version of a Transporter. She was leaning against the wall and had a book in her hand.

Luna appeared to be a child and had short curly hair with matching little pony tails on either side of her head and her bangs hanging in her eyes. She had little white flowers stuck into one ponytail, thick glasses with black frames, and tiny star earrings. She was wearing a green and white little Lolita style dress and a Transporter around her neck.

Mari looked similar but her bangs were pulled back and she had longer pieces of hair hanging in front of her ears. She was wearing a white sundress with green trimming and had a white necklace with three blue gems that served as her Transporter. She was holding a white rose and had a pair of white glasses and a halo above her head. She was the picture of innocence.

Ivy in contrast irradiated pure evil. She was wearing all black and had very pale skin. She was dressed as an assassin complete with katana and had her hair pulled back in a tight braid out of the way. She had a scar running across one eye and a pair of black cat ears on top of her head. Her normal ears were covered in piercings and she had a black piece of cloth over her mouth and nose. She, like Anna, was leaning against the wall but she was sharpening some throwing knives.

Jordan was sitting backwards in a chair with her arms resting on the back. Her hair was cut in a long bob, framing her face, with the rest of it up in a high ponytail. She had black lines under her eyes, like a football player and a green safari jacket with a brown strap running over one shoulder over a black tanktop and black skintight pants. She had a necklace with animal fangs on it as well as her Transporter. She couldn't be mistaken for anything other than a rebel.

Lastly, Simon was a typical teenage boy. He had on a green hoodie and black skinny jeans with a blue gem earring hanging from his left ear. He had a scar running diagonally across his face and over his nose and he had some stubble along his upper lip and chin.

Starlight took all this in stride within seconds and smiled. "Hi guys. Nice to meet you all. I've got a proposition for you all."

"What's that?" Jordan asked adjusting her weight on the chair.

"You can all see what's happening in the real world right? Assuming that this is the inside of my mind."

"Yup," Simon grinned and pointed to the balcony doors. They were open but beyond that the world was black. "When someone is awake and controlling our body it's like a window. We see and hear what you do."

"Cool," Starlight grinned. "Then you know what my friends and I are trying to do right?"

"Yup," Trouble laughed. "And it should work. I volunteer Anna and Chase for this operation. They're the most suited for your parents' personalities. Chase can keep his cool and is good with business. Anna is the perfect government worker."

"Wait Chase is dude?" Starlight asked.

"I can be either and really have no preference," Chase shrugged.

"Oh, okay then."

"Why can't I go out?" Ivy asked, her voice quiet and menacing.

"Because you're a homicidal maniac and don't care what or who gets in the way," Trouble said.

"Please don't let her out," the younger girls said in unison.

"We won't," Anna reassured them. "Alright, let's get going, we don't want to waste any more time."

"Wait how long has it been?" Starlight asked.

"About five hours in the real world." Jordan said casually.

"What?! But I've only been here for a few minutes!" Starlight protested.

"Yeah time is weird here. It took you forever to take in all the details and process everything. What you're looking at right now is what your brain is letting you see because you're used to processing things this way," Anna explained. "The more you come here, and the more practice you get in, the slower time will move outside."

"Oh. Okay," Starlight said. "And what's through those doors?" She pointed to the doors leading to the hallway.

"Our rooms, your memories, the rest of your mind. Be careful it's a maze in there." Trouble warned.

"Right okay, memories. I really need to do something about them. There's too many," Starlight mused.

"Yeah, sure but later, we gotta go now!" Chase said. "Just walk through the balcony doors. Let Anna go first."

They did and soon the screen turned on. Anna was looking at a worried Robert. "Oh! Hey guys! She's awake! Luna, how you feeling?"

"I'm fine, and I'm not Luna. I'm Anna. Luna is still inside. I'm supposed to pretend to be her mom."

Inside everyone looked at Luna then Starlight. The little girl was blushing furiously. "They do that every time!" she complained.

"Sorry," Starlight said. "It was all I could think of at the time."

Outside Robert got the connection ready "Oh okay, then we'll start the transfer stage. Hang on," he said.

A minute later the screen when black again and Chase stepped forward, "Okay my turn. You go after me Star." He walked through the doors and the screen lit up.

"I'm Chase," he said, answering Robert's question. "Sta- I mean Luna is coming next."

The screen went black again and Starlight stepped forward. "Well, see you guys then," she waved and stepped through. Opening her eyes, she looked around and saw Robert leaning over her.

"Luna?"

"Yeah, I'm good."

"Okay, you didn't say your alters were coming out first. You had us worried."

"I'm sorry. But everything's set up now, right?" she asked.

"Yup, here are Mr. and Mrs. Newman." Robert gestured to the Holo-me's standing on the other side of the room. "Your alters sure are good."

"Thanks. Hey Anna, Chase, how are things?"

"We're good," Anna said. She shook her head, still unused to having her own body to control. The Holo-me's were projected from a gem on, in this case, a necklace and could sustain themselves for over a week without external energy.

"Weird but good," Chase added.

"It works!" Robert grinned. "It actually works!"

"Yeah you made it, of course it works." Starlight grinned. "Not all my stuff works on the first try though. Oh yeah you guys are just in time for lunch. Jake and Rose are already in the kitchen. Uh... you two might want to stay down here," he told the alters, eyeing their jerky and awkward movements, "And practice."

The projected, semi solid, alter-controlled holograms nodded. "Sure, good idea. Come on Chase, let's walk around."

The next day also dawned bright and early. The alters and Rose has stayed the night at Starlight's house and took a tour of the house as well as learning everything they needed to know about being Mr. and Mrs. Newman. Hopefully, if all went according to plan, Rose's parents would only stay for a few hours at most. Personally Starlight and Rose were hoping for less than a half an hour.

Amber and Stefin arrived right on schedule and the Holo-me's greeted them at the door. Anna and Chase performed perfectly- shaking hands, answering questions, and asking all the right ones.

"Wow, Luna," Rose whispered as the adults went into the kitchen. "Those guys were in your head?"

"Yup, I'm pretty awesome if I do say so myself."

All in all Operation Meet the Parents was a success. Amber seemed to buy the act and Stefin was happy that Amber was happy. The couple left with several freshly baked goods and an invite to come over anytime they happened to be home. Which the girls knew to be never.

"Great job guys. Uh…"

"Time to go back in your head?" Anna grinned.

"Well, yeah. Robert says I can keep the Holo-me's though. They might come in handy later. So you can visit the real world more often," Starlight said enthusiastically.

"That's great! Just never let Ivy out, 'kay?" Chase warned.

"I know, don't worry. You guys can't get out unless there's no one driving right?"

"Yup. See ya *Luna*," the genderbender teased.

"Bye kid," Anna smiled. They each took a hold of Starlight's hands and transferred themselves back into her mind. Rose was quick to pick up the fallen projection necklaces.

"I'd say that was a job well done," Rose laughed.

"Yup, gotta love those guys."

"How many are there?"

"Uh… eight so far as I'm aware."

"And who's Ivy?"

"The evil one."

"Oh. Yeah then don't let her out."

"Not planning to. What do you say about going out for ice cream?"

"Count me in!"

✪ ✪ ✪

Joshua was planning with Erak. Even with Saniya putting a Time spell on him, he was taking forever. This person had to be at this exact spot at this exact time, etcetera. He rubbed his head and tried to make sense of the General's complicated plans. They were going to attack Planet Four. It was a big move that would gain them control of the Portals as well as making a good base for their main operations.

"Erak, don't you think you're taking this a bit too seriously?" Loki asked with glee, sounding exactly like Joshua.

"No *Commander* Flame. I don't." Erak growled not looking up from his work.

Joshua closed his eyes, this day could only get worse.

✪ ✪ ✪

"Okay guys, I've got something important to tell you," Starlight began. Several years had passed and she, Rose, and Robert were sitting at her kitchen table. "I know you two are planning on getting married and I have to ask you a favor."

"Okay, what is it?" Robert asked.

"There's this government secret I'm going to tell you. You know the Atlantis Princess, Star?"

"Yes."

"Well, she's a Blender. I know you both know what that is. She's still alive and she needs a new family." She continued to tell them all about the princess's history. "So now she's going to start a new cycle in a few months and she needs someone to take her. Usually the government just picks a random family but she told me she wanted you guys to take her."

"And she knows us because..." Rose asked.

"She's a friend of mine and I told her about you," Starlight grinned.

"Oh, okay."

"Yeah. Robert, I need you to give her the new Transporter as soon as you get her. She'll need it. Oh and set the password to activation code."

"Is this one of your... 'I just know' moments?" Robert asked.

"Yup, so trust me on this one."

"Okay. We'll take her, and give her the extra Transporter. Anything else?" Rose smiled at her fiancé.

"Yeah, I have to go soon, stuff to see, people to do and all that." She grinned at Robert.

"I'm rubbing off on you," he shook his head.

"Yep. And I need the plans and the prototype for your Bubbleshield."

"What? Why? I've just started-"

"I know, just trust me on this one. I'll give it back."

"Alright..." he acquiesced.

"Good, I'll stop by your place and pick them up on my way out."

"Where are you going?" Rose asked.

"Places. But I'll be back for your wedding," Starlight promised with a heavy heart. The Darkist would attack a few days before their wedding. Robert would be captured and Rose most likely killed. *No, I won't let that happen!* she vowed. *I'm not just going to let Rose die.* Unfortunately for the sake of history, Robert would still have to be captured. *But we'll come and rescue you.* She'd do whatever it took. Until then she had places to be.

CHAPTER 22

The place was just like she remembered. Tiny, dirty, and stuffed full of computers and tech. Its occupant looked up from her work on the screen. "And you are?" Katie asked annoyed.

"The name is Anna. I understand you're working on an Artificial Intelligence unit?"

"Yes, how do you know?" the blonde snapped.

"I work with R&R and I'm trying to do something about their leadership issues. I've got a whole new place set up, people willing to be in charge, but we have a tiny issue. The Darkist have a Time Demon under their control and we need a way to track it. Plus we have a few Blenders that need something to keep track of their memories for them."

"Uh huh." Katie nodded skeptically. "Let's just say I do believe your crazy claim for a minute. How do you plan on powering this thing? To make something that big and complicated, you'd need a huge power source."

"Power's not an issue. You're using Portal Crystals, but it's not enough- you need more."

"There's nothing more powerful than a Portal Crystal." Katie argued.

"Yes there is... More Portal Crystals."

159

"You claim to have over a thousand Portal Crystals?" Katie raised an eyebrow. The two were sitting in Katie's hideout. "First- where did you get them, and second- how are you *containing* them all? Even one Crystal is equal to about nine hundred *petawatts* and you have A THOUSAND OF THEM?!"

"There's more where that came from. I was only able to harvest a thousand before I had to leave, but I can go back at any time."

"You mean there's MORE?!" Katie said incredulously. "*All in one place*?!"

"Yes. And don't worry, no one else can get their hands on them. I've got security measures, but the AI would come in really handy..."

"When do we start?" Katie jumped in.

"Okay, so most of its done already. Right here we have your basic AI computer. I got the plans from a guy named Robert Gilgalad, so I just followed the instructions. What do you need it to be able to do?" Katie asked as she sat back and observed her work.

"Oh you know, just keep people from stealing the Crystals, store our blender's memories, track two Time Demons, run the headquarters plus it's defenses, have a cool personality, and learn."

"So it's heavy duty then?"

"Yeah pretty much. How long is it going to take to finish it?"

"A few months. This is complicated stuff here, lady. Then we'll need to install it."

"I've got that," Starlight cut in. "I just need the complicated stuff done."

"Okay," Katie got down to work while started on her own parts. "Ever think what you're going to name it? It should have a gender too. You got a voice in mind?"

"Yeah, I've got something." Starlight grinned. "It's gonna be a dude named Larry."

Katie stopped what she was doing and gave Starlight a weird look. "You're going to call it *Larry*? What, does it stand for something?"

"No," Starlight frowned. "It's just Larry. What's wrong with Larry?"

"Nothing, nothing... Just, *Larry* doesn't sound like an AI that's all."

"Does it have to? Anything can be a name. I read about these two twins named Coke and Pepsi-"

"What?"

"It's an Earth thing," Starlight mumbled. "Never mind. My point is, it stops being weird if you're used to calling someone that. Ain't nothing wrong with Larry, 'cept you're not used to it."

"Whatever you say lady." Katie turned back to her work and shook her head.

Soon Larry, as he came to be called, was ready to be tested. "Hey lady, he's done for now."

"Cool," Starlight grinned.

"We should test him out before you take him away though."

"Don't want me to leave with your baby?" Starlight teased.

"Whatever, we have really crappy stuff here so he won't be able to see much. Does this headquarters of yours have-"

"It's got cameras, speakers, and sensors of all kind in every nook and cranny." Starlight grinned. "There's nowhere he can't go."

"Right. I'm coming to visit him later."

"That's fine. In fact I'm counting on it. Alright, let's fire him up."

The first thing the being called Larry became aware of was a girl. She introduced herself as Anna, but his programing and the sensor implanted into his hard drive said her name was Star of Atlantis. He was about to say so but was interrupted by the introduction of another girl named Katie. Again his information was different. Her name was Katie Boardo.

"Larry, the first you need to know, is that most people aren't addressed by their full names," Katie said, anticipating his question.

"Oh. Alright. I shall call you Katie then. And I shall call you Anna."

"He's a little stiff," Katie frowned.

"I'll work with him," Starlight said. "Now that we know he works. I'll install him in HQ. Come on Larry, we have some work to do."

The girls shut him down for travel and Starlight grabbed all the tech he came with, preparing to leave. "Be careful with him," Katie sniffed.

"Don't worry. I will." Starlight did one last check over then disappeared from the hideout.

✪ ✪ ✪

The place was far underground and very hard to reach. Starlight had a hard time finding it in the first place, then getting past the defenses had been harder. The Darkist had all manner of security, including Soulforce detectors. She would show up on their scans no matter what she did, so she improvised.

"Message, Kapital City, Planet Four, Isis Dimension, Kegan the Portalshroom."

On the other side of the shield, Kegan spazzed out at the hologram that had appeared.

"Kegan, this is Starlight, I'm sure you remember me. I've got an important job for you. You see that lever?" the apparition pointed to Kegan's right. Kegan's eyes darted over to the right hand wall, then back to the hologram.

"It's a fire alarm, I need you pull it."

Kegan glanced at the lever then back to the hologram several times.

"The guards here say you're a mushroom, don't you want to set them straight?"

Kegan blinked and narrowed his eyes. "I. AM. NOT. A. MUSHROOOOOOOM!" he yelled and flew at the lever. The alarms went off and Starlight grinned. *Good old Kegan.* As soon as everyone inside had left the safety of the shield, she grabbed Kegan on his way out and Transported them both out of there.

Kegan looked around warily. They were at the bottom of the, by now, familiar hill. Starlight grinned and raised her eyebrows, inclining her head towards the stairs. Kegan eyed her up and down, hovering in place. "Kegan, I've another job for you."

"What?" he snapped, his face still read for his latest mushroom episode.

"What's the biggest Portal Crystal Cache you've ever guarded?"

"That one you just kidnapped me from!" Kegan spat. "They had forty-seven Crystals!"

"Forty seven?" Starlight scoffed. "Compared to me, they have none!"

"How many did you collect?"

"Not collect, found, in their natural state."

"Where are they?"

"Right this way." Starlight took him up the stairs and stopped at the Crossroads. "You know, you're the first person to see that sign other than me." She pointed to the IDTA sign.

"Not interested, where are the Portal Crystals? I can sense them. There's a lot and they're close."

"Yes, yes they are. Come on." The redhead led him down the path and into the mist. About halfway between her construction and the Crossroads she stopped and Kegan looked around.

"There's nothing here!" He complained.

"Yes there is, you can feel them can't you?"

"Yes, but I can't *see* them!"

She grinned and took out a remote, pressing one of the buttons. The event that followed was incredible. The mist was suddenly illuminated by millions of tiny lanterns on the ground, making it almost transparent. The field under the mist extended on for miles and miles before the mist wasn't lit up, and you just *knew* that it went on far beyond that. Covering the ground in a sea of blue were trillions of Portal Crystals just growing there. It was a sight to behold.

She glanced at the Portalshroom and hid a smile. He was standing- not floating- his mouth hanging open and practically touching the ground. Then a single tear ran slowly down his red face and fell to the ground.

"You know, it's a lot of Crystals for just one Portalshroom... Think you'd be willing to be in charge of a few others?"

The question immediately turned his attention away from his prize. Portalshrooms were very territorial and didn't get along with each other very well. He seemed to consider the question seriously though. "How many more?" he asked suspiciously.

"Uh... how many would you suggest?"

"Two. Only two more."

"That stingy huh?"

"I am not stingy you red-haired monster!" he looked on the verge of a ranting rage so she wisely refrained from adding any further comments.

"I'll just leave you and them *alone* for a while shall I?" she smirked and wiggled her brows, but luckily he wasn't paying any attention.

"Yes, yes good idea. I'll stay here and guard the Crystals. You go do... whatever." he made his way into the field and proceeded to ignore her.

"I'm putting the Forcefield up while I'm gone okay. Don't try to cross the path... Oh never mind, he'll figure it out," she ended with a shrug. She shook her head and left him to his new paradise. She still had some finishing touches to add to her construction.

CHAPTER 23

She grinned and quickly made her way to Earth-235. Her vacation was over and it was time to get back in the game. This time, she appeared on the north side the town. She watched as the past Starlight appeared and made her way to the tavern, followed by the Time Demon, Saniya. The redhead waited outside the tavern door until Saniya came back outside and held up her hands.

"Hey Sanyia. Look! See! I didn't send myself forward in Time, and I figured out how to make your master mortal again!" She said quickly. "I'm back in business."

"My Master isn't mortal *yet,* creature."

"Yeah, but just wait! Cause- you see, you sent me back about five thousand years and back then, in five thousand years- nowish- Joshua will have the choice to give up his immortality."

"He will not choose that." Sanyia interrupted.

"No! Yes he will! I've just spent the last *five thousand years* making his life miserable! I've driven him insane! Okay look. The Darkist are planning to attack R&R in a few days. A few days after that, is the day Joshua has to make his choice. His options are getting slim and he's scared. I've got him cornered and he knows it. One more push and he won't be able to take it anymore. That's why I'm here getting my last guy."

"Then I will give you ten days. If he isn't mortal by then you will not have fulfilled your end of the bargain and I must carry out my Master's orders."

"Ten days... Okay I can work with this. Good, perfect. Okay, see you around. Oh and try not to mess with my plans because this is for your benefit as well." Starlight nodded and waved, darting into the tavern.

Sanyia nodded at the closing door and vanished. Inside Starlight walked back over to her corner table and sat down, glancing at the bartender. He just glared at her, still completely unconcerned, and continued to wipe the glass with his dirty rag. She smiled into the table. Some things just never changed.

Eventually the strains of battle died down and the sounds of glorious victory filled the air. Apparently the locals had either killed or driven off their attackers. The tavern soon filled as the warriors had their injuries attended to and came in for some well-earned celebrating. She kept her eyes on the door and waited for her friend to come in.

Loki soon made an appearance, coming in with a group of warriors. His golden blonde hair was short for the area, but still long for a male, with two longer pieces hanging down to his chest in front of his ears. His eyes were a light green and he was wearing a dark green tunic under his leather armor. His knives were slung at his belt and he had a small hunting bow at his back.

He scanned the room, saw her waving, and excused himself from his friends. "Star! Long time no see. How've you been?"

"I've been good. But how've you been? The Battle of Idiots?"

"Yeah," he laughed, sitting down across from her. "They were idiots. So what's up? What are the Darkist doing now?"

"Uh, well. I've gotten some new information since I last talked to you. They're planning on attacking the last few places they haven't yet, including R&R."

"Star," Loki sighed. "You know I don't like the R&R."

"I know, but I've got a plan. How do you feel about Time travel? I've got a job for you."

"Go on..."

"There's this guy I know that needs a shadow. Oh, and try not to let him sleep..."

✪ ✪ ✪

They all gathered at the landing pad of the spaceport for the Captain's arrival. Everyone but Arya seemed to be justifiably nervous. The elf simply looked bored. As the ship descended into the atmosphere, Lester gave a shout and all eyes were trained on the flying vessel. The sails were being drawn in and people hurried about the deck, getting ready to dock.

The ship seemed to be coming in too fast and the people waiting on the pad watched with baited breath. The Captain was at the helm and he was grinning like a madman. Closer and closer the ship came with no signs of slowing. Then, just when it seemed it would crash into the port, the engines cut out and with a skillful twist of the wheel, the ship pulled up next to the landing pad and stopped, hovering.

The gangway was lowered and people started making their way down, Dare among them. He leapt onto the landing pad and immediately made his way over to the welcome committee. "Hey Robert! Glad to see you guys made it out."

"Yep, heard you ran into some trouble," Robert laughed.

"Yeah, Trouble's a good lass, that one is." The Captain had come up behind Dare. "Captain Alastor Azazel. And yeh all must be the motley crew."

"Arya Greylance. Don't currently have a rank, but I guess I'm something like a general," The elf said and held out her hand. The Captain took it in a truce like gesture and signaled his crew to disembark.

"Pleasure Miss Greylance. So yah have a plan?"

"It's in the making. We'll probably have to regroup with the R&R; they have better defenses there."

"Good thinkin'. Any word from Miss Trouble?"

"He means Starlight," Dare explained. "Apparently she introduced herself as Trouble."

"Great but we can talk about this inside. Captain, how many of your crew or passengers can pilot a fighter ship?"

They had all gathered inside when the call came in. The Darkist were on the move. "Alright everybody, we'd better get moving," Arya commanded. "Captain, get your people ready to go, we move out in two hours."

"Aye General Greylance."

"Katie, Ben, and Scott- I want you to organize the pilots. Get them ready to fly by the time we leave." They nodded and hurried off to complete their jobs. "Dare, Gil- I need you to get this place ready to fly. Close all the extremities and grab a team to fly guard."

"Wait, we're taking the spaceport?" Lester asked incredulously.

"Yes. Lester, you're in charge of making sure everyone has a uniform. I want everyone equipped when we get there."

"Okay, the R&R ones?"

"What other uniforms do we have?" She asked.

"Right, right. Just checking. Okay I'm on it!" Lester ran to complete his task.

"And what will we be doing?" Jake asked.

"Can either of you fly?"

"No..."

"Then I need you here. Robert you know how to fly this hunk of metal, don't ya?"

"In theory. But-"

"That's good enough for me," Arya cut in. "We're working on a tight schedule here. Jake, I need you here with me relaying orders."

"Sure. Need anything else?" he asked.

"Yeah, a way to get rid of the Darkist."

"Can't help you there."

"I know, alright people, let's get to work."

The R&R headquarters was in shambles. Alarms were going off, people were running around and no one could decide what to do. Some people had suited up and were manning the battle stations, others were hiding in rooms and hallways, others still were just running around being useless. People started panicking anew when a fleet of ships and their command center entered the atmosphere.

As the fighter ships landed and people started to disembark the Captain's ship, Arya looked around at the disorder and chaos and sighed. This wouldn't do. At all. She gathered her commanders and advanced upon the R&R command center. Inside the 'leaders' were cowering or arguing. When the elf princess came barreling in, and started barking out orders no one questioned her except one of the more dimwitted fellows.

"Why should we listen to you?"

"Because if you don't, you'll die," she said simply. He seemed to get it and was banished along with the rest of them. Their choices- stay and fight or run and get shot down by the enemy when they got here. Apparently some decided the risk was worth it as one of the ships took off into the atmosphere, heading for safety. "Fools. Only safety they'll get was staying here."

"Well," Gil's tone was light. "They're dead."

Arya ignored him and grabbed hold of the speaker, turning off the alarms. "R&R." Her strong voice boomed through every speaker on the premises. "Congratulations, you now have new leadership. As of right now there is no Rebels or Resistance, only the R&R. The Darkist are closing in and have already begun to attack the last free areas. The first order you will receive is *stop panicking*. Secondly, everyone get to your posts, *now*. Full battle uniform. Wait until your new division head gives you the orders to advance. Now *get moving!*"

"Wow, you can practically *feel* the righteousness surging through-" Lester was interrupted when his sister whacked him over the head.

"Report to you stations," she told the group. "Your soldiers are waiting."

Chapter 24

Previously

Loki looked at his watch. Tormenting Joshua had been fun but it was time to catch up with Star now. He regretfully left the horrendously sleep deprived immortal and made his way to meet his friend. She was waiting right where he had left her, sitting in the corner of that tavern waiting for him.

To the bartender- who had seen everything and kept an eye on the redhaired girl in the corner- someone did the vanishing trick again. No sooner did the victorious blonde disappear, only to walk in through the door again. Magic was generally frowned upon in his village so it wasn't often you saw someone openly doing magical things.

Starlight grinned as Loki came in and sat back down. "Did you have fun?"

"Very. What now?" he asked.

"Well... Now we go and join the fight."

"Which is..."

"Currently at R&R HQ."

"Ah."

"But don't worry, I'm sure my friends have worked out a new command system. You got your Transporter?" she asked.

"Yup. Shall we?"

"Yes, let's do it here, the bartender seems to be enjoying my show." She grinned and waved at the grumpy man behind the counter. He just glowered at her and continued to wipe his cup. "Activation code, R&R headquarters."

"Mischief managed, R&R headquarters."

The bartender didn't even blink.

As soon as Loki showed up at R&R Starlight grinned and said, "Mischief managed?"

"Of course."

"You don't get it, do you?"

"Get what?"

"Never mind. It's an Earth thing." She looked around and saw that there were people doing things, and it actually looked *organized*. Her friends must already be here. "Okay, let's go look for them, any suggestions?"

"By the state of things I'd say our best bet would be command."

"Command it is. You know what sucks about regular Transporters?" She asked as they started walking to the elevators. "They only transport you to the same spot in a location. For example, you could go to R&R but you'd always end up at the same spot in R&R, you can't go straight to someone's office or something."

"Yeah, but those are regular Transporters," Loki grinned.

"True..." Starlight agreed. "But we're almost there anyway so why bother."

"You'd think they'd make their command center harder to reach from the front doors. What if someone attacked?" Loki smirked.

"Well, this is *their* HQ, not ours."

"We have an HQ?"

"Not officially yet, but yeah."

"Cool, does it have cool toys?"

"Better than what they have here."

"I wanna see it!"

"Just wait, trust me."

They had reached the command center and walked through the doors. Arya and Jake were standing in front of the video feeds from around the complex watching the progress. Apparently they were too busy to notice Starlight and Loki coming up, because when the former casually walked up behind her uncle and said "boo" he jumped three feet in the air. Turning around, he caught sight of his missing niece and a huge smile broke out on his face.

"Starlight!" Sweeping her up in a bear hug, he spun her around several times before relinquishing his hold. "I've been so worried! Where have you been? What happened? Who-"

"Woah! Jake, one question at a time please!" She grinned. "Man have I missed you! Oh- this is my friend Loki. So you'll never believe this, but I've been gone longer than you think. But we'll have to wait for good explanations. Word is the Darkist are attacking."

"Yeah, Arya took over command of the R&R and everyone was too stunned to argue, but we don't know how long that's going to last. Everyone else is commanding their stations and getting ready for the bad guys' arrival."

"Okay. Arya, where do you need us?" She asked.

"I hate to say it, but right now we're sitting ducks. The Darkist forces far outnumber our own and we have no way of getting off the planet unless we fly out. There's no Portal here, security hazard, but if there was the Darkist would be blocking it. Worst case scenario, the shields break down and they just blow it all to kingdom come."

"And the least worst scenario?" Loki inquired.

"We end up surrendering before they blow us up."

"I think I can get you all a way out," Starlight grinned.

"How long will it take?"

"As long as you can hold them all off, but I'll need to borrow Robert."

"Done. Let me know the minute you have it ready."

"No problem. Can you direct me to the right place?"

"Down the hall, third door on the left."

"Thanks, see ya Jake, Loki." The redhead slipped out the doors and made her way down the hall.

Jake looked at Loki. "So you *the* Loki?"

"Seeing as there was no original Loki, and I took over the already existing reputation, then yes I suppose so."

"Cool," Jake nodded.

Out in the hall, Starlight smiled. Those two would be just fine. She knocked on the right door and walked in without waiting for a reply. Robert looked up from his desk and smiled. "Star?"

"That's me, nice to finally officially meet you." She grabbed a chair and sat down with the back between her knees. "Okay, so here's the deal. We're trapped in a kill box. Our only chance out alive is surrender or we make another way. I'm leaning toward the second option. I've got enough Portal Crystals on me to Transport the entire planet out of the way, but no way to use the energy to do it. I need your help. You built this Transporter," she took off the necklace and set it down on the desk. "Now I need you to make it bigger."

He looked at her, thinking hard. "I think we can get all the materials, but we'll have to set it up all over the perimeter of this place."

"Right. And try not to get killed once the fighting starts."

"Exactly. I'm going to need a few things."

"I can get you anything you need. Oh, and thanks for agreeing to take me in. Really appreciate it."

The inventor nodded and handed her a list of things to get. "Hurry back as soon as you get it all. I'll start working with the stuff I have in here."

She nodded and left the room. *Let's do this!*

✪ ✪ ✪

Erak Darke looked over his army. His fleet was the most advanced highest quality, his troops were professionally trained highly dangerous soldiers, and his plan was unbeatable. Unfortunately the R&R had better. But they were trapped and their leadership was nonexistent. He had already taken Zilos and the other free places that could actually stand against him. He had Joshua working out all the political bits while he focused on the military aspect of it.

They were on their way to the R&R, tracking the ship his operatives had found. An insider had anonymously confirmed that the ship was indeed located at the secret headquarters. They were just coming upon the solar system when his top commander came in to report their progress.

"Sir, our man has confirmed that Starlight is inside R&R. They have nowhere to run. Our troops are moving into position now. They have their shields up, but they should be down soon. Our man is on the job as we speak. He also reported that they have a new leader who actually knows what she's doing." Joshua stood at attention as he relayed the information.

"Very good. As soon as we are done here I want a dimension wide broadcast that the ΖΣЯΘs is ours. Let it be known that their salvation is at hand. We will take its imperfections and create a new perfect existence."

"Those exact words, General?"

"Yes. Work out the details." Erak looked at his subordinate and frowned. "Joshua, your state of personal appearance is usually much better than this. Still can't sleep?"

"No sir. However I'm perfectly capable of commanding this battle."

They both turned towards the door as a messenger hurried in. "Their shields are down, Sir. However they have their own fleet ready," the man gasped and hunched over to catch his breath.

"Sir?" Joshua looked at the General, his eyes gleaming.

"Send in the first volley," the Darkist leader said. "To let them know we're here."

CHAPTER 25

The explosions rocked the whole headquarters, sending waves crashing onto the floating habitat. In the control center Arya smiled grimly. "Hello to you too. Our forces are on standby, correct?"

"Yes," Jake nodded. "Why aren't our shields up?"

"It appears we have a traitor in our midst," she shook her head.

"Who?"

Arya pointed to one of the screens on the far wall. Ben was cornered in front of the shield's generators, some stray R&R guards holding him at gunpoint. He looked very smug as smoke drifted up from the generators behind him.

"*Ben*? But why? He-"

"I've heard Darkist spies are well paid," the elf sighed. "I just never thought Ben would take the bait. We've been drifting apart ever since he came back from his last tour on my home planet. He was just different- hid it very well, but I noticed. He probably ran into them around that time and they struck a deal. He was never one to go for the money though."

"Is he the only one?"

"We have no way of knowing. All we can do is hold them off for as long as possible to give Starlight and your brother time to get us out of here." She ordered the guards to bring him up.

The next batch of explosions brought their attention back to the main screens. Their satellites had orbited into the right position and what they depicted looked grim. Hundreds of Darkist ships were moving into position, readying their guns. There were five battle ships placed at strategic places amongst the smaller fighter ships and at the back of the fleet was the main command ship. All were the signature Darkist shades of black and grey. They were lined up in perfect order, not one ship out of place.

Arya rolled her eyes. "Only Erak."

"What do we do?" Jake asked.

"Fire back. But not yet."

"What, why not?"

"Jake, if you're going to be my top commanding officer then you need to stop asking why to everything I say. If I want you to know then I'll tell you," Arya said patiently. "We've got some pretty big guns here just in case of attack. But they take a while to warm up. If we let the Darkist get a few more hits in without retaliating then we can use the guns to target the whole fleet. If they don't break ranks then most of them will be gone and we won't be so drastically outnumbered. We may stand a chance."

"Oh, ok." He had the decency to look sheepish. "How is Star and Robby's progress going?"

"Take a look," she brought up Robert's improvised workshop and kept track of Starlight's movements through various cameras. His brother was tinkering with a very large amount of Portal Crystals, attaching a metal device to each glowing blue stone. He had on a pair of thick gloves to protect his hands from the energy coming off the Crystals and his hair was slightly standing on end as if there was a lot of static electricity in the air. On Starlight's screen the redhead rushed around collecting anything resembling a stick or pole along with several other oddly shaped items.

She had multiple guns hanging from a belt around her waist which clanked together as she ran.

The third set of explosions came a few seconds after and Arya grabbed hold of the microphone. "Loki, how much longer do the guns need?"

"159, 158, 157-" his voice came over the speakers.

"Great as soon as they're ready, fire at will."

"Sweet!"

"How are your men handling things guys?" the elf addressed the rest of her newly appointed officers.

'Surprising well' was the overall response. The princess nodded and set her attention on the person leading the fighter ships. "Scott, once Loki has taken his shot, I want your guys to advance. Don't engage. Focus all your attention on dodging their shots. I need you to get in and get personal. Take the fight to them. We have civilians here, families with children. We need to protect the habitat at all costs."

"Roger that."

"Gil, Dare, I need your men on standby. If the enemy breaks through the atmosphere you have permission to engage."

"Understood."

"Lester, if they make it to the surface, same goes for you. Scott, how high up can the shnorkelfooses jump?"

"About a quarter of a mile."

The elf raised her eyebrows. "Wow."

"Yeah they're pretty big," he grinned.

"Robert, how's it coming?"

"Good, as soon as Starlight gets back I can finish putting these things together. Then we'll go set them up." The inventor wiped his forearm over his brow. The pressure was starting to get to him.

"Katie, any luck with their communications?"

"Not yet," the blonde replied. "Their codes are very complicated. But we'll break through soon enough."

"Good. Await further orders. Loki?"

"Four, three, two... and fire!" the whole habitat shook as he fired an enormous pulse dead center into the Darkist's fleet. The results were immediate and terrible. The entire center was completely obliterated with debris flying into the surrounding ships. Only the right and left wings were still in position and they were heavily damaged. The blast had taken out three of the five battle ships but hadn't so much as scratched the command vessel. More than two thirds of the entire fleet had been destroyed however they still outnumbered the R&R three to one.

As they started to recover from the R&R's retaliation strike, scrambling to present a uniform face, Arya smiled. "Take that you-"

✪ ✪ ✪

Erak smiled. "Their main guns are out of commission now. Bring out the rest of the force. Perhaps they'll decide to surrender."

✪ ✪ ✪

Arya's eye widened and she broke off mid-sentence. More ships had started to appear into the visible spectrum. When before they had numbered in the hundreds, now there were thousands of them. They had been shielding until this moment, waiting for their cue. They appeared out of nowhere much closer than the previous lineup and were entering the atmosphere as they appeared, their shields burning off as they raced towards the planet's watery surface.

"Gil! Dare! Deploy your men now! Don't let them reach the surface. Get them into shnorkelfoose range if you can. Scott, keep them occupied."

"Yes ma'am!" They could be heard barking orders as their divisions flew to meet the attacking force.

"Lester, get ready. Make sure none of them get a chance to land or hit anything. Dare will keep the skies directly overhead clear. Loki, go check the evacuation. Make sure all civilians are in the lowest regions of the habitat. They'll be the safest there."

Loki nodded and ran to round up the last remaining stragglers.

"Starlight?" Arya's voice was tight.

"Almost there. We've got the pieces and are almost done assembling." The redhead grabbed several of the finished pieces and at Robert's order, darted out of the room. Racing down the stairs, she started placing the large spikes into the metal of the habitat. Soon her path crossed Loki's and she handed him several of the spikes giving him instructions.

"Take these down to the bottom of the habitat. Jam them into the walls where the refugees are. I'll take the top floors and the outside," she said.

"Are you crazy?" Loki asked.

"Blender, remember? I can't die. I'll be fine."

"But you can still get hurt."

"Then I'll hurt them back. Hurry, we don't have much time before they reach the surface. By the time they get here I want to be long gone."

The blonde trickster nodded and continued into the depths of the habitat. On his way down, he found a few more civilians and directed them to the right place. This time when the explosions hit, pieces of the habitat started to fall down around him. This far down, the destruction shouldn't have been so bad. He couldn't imagine what damage the upper levels had suffered. A cry from one of the rooms drew his attention.

He dashed to the room, kicking the locked door down. Two blonde haired children were desperately trying to pull something out of a pile of wreckage. "Hey," he called. The girl turned around and saw him giving him a pleading look. "Can you help our brother? He's stuck!" Her brother turned around and nodded. They were twins, about twelve years old.

He nodded motioning the children back and scouted out the area, making sure to locate all the possible collapse points. He put his spikes down and extended his hands. They watched in awe as he mentally lifted the rubble. "Pull him out," he commanded. The children nodded and hurried forward to pull their brother out of the mess. He came out feet first with several badly bleeding injuries. He was very pale and had black hair. His eyes were closed and he appeared to be unconscious.

Loki quickly checked him over and decided that he could be moved. "My name's Loki," he said, picking up the limp teenager and walking out of the room. The twins picked up his spikes and hurried after him.

"I'm Luke and this is Lucy. That's our older brother David," the boy said.

"Okay, are your parents here?"

"No, but our oldest brother Liam is here somewhere," the girl said worried.

"I'm sure he's down with the rest of the civilians." The trickster led the twins down the last few flights of stairs and onto the lowest floor. Pillars attached the ceiling to the floor which was made of glass, the ocean floor just visible far below it. The walls were also made of glass and curved making the whole room shaped like an upside down dome. Covering the surface of the thick glass was another smaller shield, protecting the room from the shnorkelfooses and attack. Hundreds of people were packed into the massive hall. The twins scanned the faces of everyone there, looking for their older brother while Loki brought his charge to the medic station.

"Lucy! Luke!" The shout came from a tan skinned young man with long curling black hair and piercing blue eyes. He had a pair of black glasses which he took off as the twins dive bombed him in a group hug. He embraced them and the three of them hurried over to the medic station. "David, is he alright?"

"He's a little beat up and his arm is broken but he's going to be fine," one of the medics assured him.

Liam nodded and turned to Loki. "Thank you. You rescued my family."

"It's no problem." Loki shrugged. "The name is Loki."

"Liam, nice to meet you." The two shook hands and Loki turned to the twins.

"I'm going to need the spikes back now."

"What are they for?" Lucy asked as she and her brother handed them over.

"Honestly I don't know. Just that they'll get all of us out of here before the Darkist decide to blow us up." He frowned looking around for a place to put them. The only available options were the metal columns. He did as Starlight had asked and rammed the four of them soundly into the metal. People looked up to watch what he was doing, but no one asked about them. As soon as the last one was in place he activated his mic and told the redhead that everything was good to go.

She thanked him and continued with her mission. She was just about to head out into the open with the final spikes when the call came in. Scott was dead.

CHAPTER 26

Gil's eyes had glazed over. Scott was dead. Scott was dead? He couldn't be dead. His longtime friend was gone. Shot out of the sky by some stupid Darkist ship. The fighting was directly overhead. People were crashing left and right, some of the enemy ships had managed to land and ground troops were spilling out, and Lester's division was running to meet them. The eel-like shnorkelfooses were jumping up from the water and taking incredibly large bites out of all the enemy ships. The splashes they created made it look like mines were going off under the surface, causing geysers of water cascading into the air. But Gil hardly noticed any of it. His best friend was gone.

He could hear Arya yelling at him to get a grip but everything seemed far away as if removed from reality. Scott had been like a younger brother to him. His race lived longer than most and though Gil knew he would die eventually, the man was still young for his kind. The rest of his life had been stolen from him in one dick move by a Darkist pilot. He didn't notice when his grief turned to rage. Didn't notice when he left off an enormous wave of energy, frying anything nearby to a crisp. Totaled enemy ships fell into the water leaving his section of sky clear.

His hands were slack on the controls of his ship, and he was going down. He didn't care. "Yes, yes you damn well do!" The voice was annoying in his head and vaguely female. "Gil snap out of it!"

Arya watched as Gil went down muttering about giving up, crashing into one of the bigger enemy craft that had managed to land, scattering the soldiers. "Whoever's outside, get Gil out of there!" she commanded.

"On it!" Starlight's voice came through the speakers. "I'm almost finished up here, just need to set these last five spikes and we're good to go. Arya, call everyone down. Send out a surrender signal. By the time they're ready to make demands we should be long gone."

"Okay, I'm going to trust you on this one. Lester, Dare- get your men out of there! Katie?"

"We've already sent the signal. I've hacked into their main ship and sent the message personally. They want our Portal Crystals, that's why they didn't just start by annihilating the whole planet." Katie informed her. "We may have a chance now. He's agreed to call back his air support. But his ground troops stay to ensure our co-operation."

Arya thanked the techie and glanced over at Ben. He was sitting in a corner, hands tied, with Dare making sure he didn't go anywhere. "Ben. Why?"

"They said they'd leave our world alone," he mumbled. "That we wouldn't have to-"

"Ben listen to yourself! This is Erak Darke we're talking about! He's crazy! There's *no* way that he'd agree to overlook a few planets."

"It wasn't Erak I made the deal with. It was Joshua. He's never going to let Erak carry out his psycho plans! They're just going to be supreme leader and all that." Ben's voice was resigned.

Arya shook her head in disgust and turned back to the screens. She pointedly ignored him and focused her attention on watching the action outside. Starlight had driven two of the five spikes into the ground and was en route to Gil. Lester was evacuating his men and was one of the last to head inside. Pausing at the door, he looked over to Starlight who waved him off telling him to get inside. Dare had taken over command of Gil's division and was leading a small strike to let everyone else get inside.

The Darkist had already given the fall back order and the majority of their ships had disengaged but a few were still stubbornly fighting on. Erak was going to be pissed about that. The third spike was set and Starlight was just helping Gil up. He was badly injured and had lost most of his left arm. She was doing her best to patch him up, but knew he was going to be fine. Blenders couldn't die. He could always regrow the arm anyway. She took the long way around as explosions still rocked the habitat, driving in the last two spikes. "Dare! Get in here!"

"I'm a little busy at the moment!" he grunted. Only four of the remaining fifteen ships he had led were left but the skirmish was soon over as the fall back order was repeated and both sides turned back. The four of them had just turned around and were flying back when one of the opposing ship 'accidentally' sent a missile. It hit the ship to Dare's left, the explosion clipping his wing. A big chunk of it was torn off and he started spiraling out of control, crashing into the ship to his right. The ship in front of him shared a similar fate and all four went down.

The nose of his ship hit the edge of the habitat and it flipped through the air, coming to a skidding halt by the other end of the tarmac. Starlight, who had just dropped Gil into the waiting arms of Lester inside the door, changed course and ran to Dare's ship. The front end was smashed in, but she managed to rip the door off and look inside.

He was covered in blood, his eyes half closed staring out the window. His legs were pinned under the wreckage and his breathing was shallow but still there. "Dare! Wake up! We need to get you out of here!" she yelled at him.

He opened his eyes at the sound of her voice and smiled. "No, I'm stuck, and I'm pretty sure my neck is broken. I can't feel anything, which is a good thing I suppose," he laughed, coughing up a little blood.

"No, just hold on we-"

"Star, it's okay. Just go. The Darkist troops are looking a little antsy over there."

She followed his gaze and saw the ground troops advancing closer towards the door, making sure no one tried to leave. "But-"

"Go. Internal bleeding, and I see a light."

"Nice attempt at dramatics."

"Thank you, I try."

"Whatever. Hey, do me a favor... take a left at the Crossroads."

"What?"

"You'll know it when you see it," she said.

"Roger that." he spit out a mouthful full of blood. "Now go."

"Fine, see you later."

"Sure."

She tore herself away from the ship and her dying friend while holding her hands up. She ran with her face covered back to the entrance to avoid recognition. Erak had almost certainly instructed his troops to keep an eye out for her. Loki met her at the entrance and took in her sad countenance. "What happened?"

"Dare."

"Oh. I'm sorry."

"It's fine. Don't worry about it. How's Gil?"

"He's... not doing too good," Loki sighed. "Scott's death really hit him."

"And the battle sitch?"

"We've formally surrendered. Arya's up in the control center negotiating right now. They want all the Portal Crystals obviously, and you..."

"Me specifically or my co-operation?" she asked as they made their way up to the control center.

"I skipped out on that bit. Came to get you."

"Thanks. Are the spikes in position?"

"Yep. Hopefully the Darkist won't mess with the ones outside." He stopped her outside the door, "Oh- before you go in, Robert wanted to talk to you."

"Kay, thanks." She quickly ducked into the inventor's workshop. "Okay, what's up?"

He looked up from the portable screen he was working on and set down his tools. "Now we just need a destination, a whole lot o' luck, and the right conditions."

"Don't know about the luck, but I got the other two covered," the redhead nodded. "Anything else?"

"Pray nothing goes wrong?"

"That too. Okay," she took the screen and programed in their destination. "I'll let you know when to hit the button. I'm gonna go and watch the negotiations."

"Okay." He waved her out and went back to work.

Raised voices were coming from the control center so Starlight proceeded with caution. Lester, Katie, and Jake were standing behind Arya as she carried on a screaming match with Erak. The Darkist leader loomed on screen with his top commanders standing behind him. Starlight's arrival distracted him.

"You!" he boomed.

The redhead covered her ears. "Erak," she said in a calm level voice. "How nice to see you again. What's going on here?"

Arya cut in before he had a chance to answer. "They want us to turn over all our Portal Crystals, weapons, and you. I told him to (insert useless insult here)."

"Oo- harsh." Starlight grinned. "And why would we do that?" she addressed Erak.

"So we don't blow you up. I understand there are civilians with you," Joshua spoke up. His face was haggard and his eyes were dull, but the voice he spoke with was strong and condescending.

"Then the Portal Crystals will be blown up too and basically the whole surrounding dimension, including you." Her point was a good one.

"I noticed you attempted to take control of our systems." Erak interceded. "But if you noticed we still have control of yours. It's a simple thing to raise your shield up to contain the blast." He also made a good point.

"Yes, but then you wouldn't have the Portal Crystals."

"True, but all your friends would be dead. And we could just pick you up. You don't happen to know what became of a certain Portalshroom of ours do you?"

"Meh, your guards were calling him a mushroom. He protested."

"Enough with the banter already." Arya cut in. "Can we please get to the point."

"As I said, give us what we want, and we won't blow you up." Erak shrugged.

"Then what? We all go free? I don't think so." The elf crossed her arms.

"You *are* an annoying bunch. So, how about this? You all join us or die, and the civilians go free."

"Classic clichéd evil villain much?" Starlight rolled her eyes. "Fine, for the sake of my poor ears, Arya formally accepts the terms. Give us some time to get all your stuff."

Arya opened her mouth, but the redhead shot a glare in her direction and the commander thought better of it.

"You have ten minutes." Erak growled.

The screen shut off and everyone looked at the Blender. She shrugged and said, "We'll be long gone before they get here anyway."

"So is your escape plan ready then?" the elf asked.

"Yeah, we just need to get all the Portal Crystals first, so they don't find them."

"Well, you heard her. Go get them. How does he expect us to get *all* the weapons in ten minutes?" Arya rolled her eyes. She turned to Ben. "Maybe we should leave you here."

He just stared at her, as if thinking *now why would you do that?* Shifting his weight slightly he opened his mouth but was prevented from talking by Robert's arrival.

"Arya. When do you want to leave? The guys hanging around on the surface are getting a little trigger happy."

"Starlight wants to grab all the Crystals before we go. The Darkist will be here in less than ten."

"Okay. Where do we go? Nowhere will be safe from them indefinitely." The inventor glanced at Ben.

Before the elf could answer, everyone else came running back into the room. They all gathered around in a circle and looked to Arya. "What now?" Katie voiced the general opinion.

"We need someplace to regroup." Arya looked at Starlight. This was *her* area of expertise.

"Everyone is going to be okay." She looked specifically at Gil. "Scott is dead, but not necessarily gone. The same goes for everyone else who died here."

Something in the other Blender's subconsciousness must have heard, because he suddenly stood up on his own and blinked.

"Okay good idea," Gil addressed Arya's earlier question. "But where?"

Starlight grinned and looked around at the destruction on the screens before her. "I know a place."

CHAPTER 27

"*This* is your place?" Gil's voice was incredulous. "There's nothing here!" They were standing at the bottom of a hill, with steps leading up to the top. All of the R&R was there. People milled around confused, as their surroundings had suddenly changed. One second everyone was in the R&R headquarters, then they weren't. The general reaction was not mass hysteria, but mild confusion. Although, perhaps *mild* was putting it lightly.

"Relax! My place is farther in. This is like the front porch I guess. Come on." Starlight led the way up the stairs, explaining as she went. They soon reached the main part of the Crossroads and came to a halt.

"Now what? Gil asked, looking around. "Please don't tell me your place is down that hole."

"Nope, even better! In that mist."

"Great. Can you even *see* the end of your nose in there?"

"On the path, yes."

"And what's at the end of the path?"

"Do you *see* the sign?"

"I. D. T. A. What's that?" Gil frowned.

"It's ID-*tuh*, moron. The Inter-Dimensional Traveling Agency."

"Right and that's… what exactly?"

"Our new club house. The R&R was getting kinda old, plus they suck. IDTA is the new thing! The Darkist will never find us here and even if someone does, usually only dead people show up here so it's not like they can go tell anyone. Anyway, straight ahead is The City, and to your right you have The Hole. Heaven and Hell. I'm not sure what the Mist is for, but I've used it to cover IDTA."

"Right. And IDTA is better than the R&R tech-wise?" Gil's voice was dripping with sarcasm.

"Yes actually. It's got stuff most people only ever dream about," the redhead grinned. "The Darkist have this thing called a Soulforce detector... Well, IDTA has a Soulforce *reader.* Our security system is run by an Artificial Intelligence named Larry."

"Larry?" Katie asked suddenly.

"Yes, the one you and *Anna* *cough* *me* *cough* made." She grinned. "I'll explain once we get inside. Come on everyone! Take a left at the Crossroads."

The Blender led the way into the mist with the whole of R&R following. Along the way she could hear people exclaiming things like, "Bob you're here! But you're supposed to be dead!" and "I know, I am."

"What exactly is this place?" Gil asked. He couldn't help but hear the reunions and his face had a nervous hopeful expression.

"I think it's an in-between place where you can decide where you want to go. Like I said, typically only dead people show up here so all the guys that died in the battle popped up here. I guess they just blended into the crowd. Scott's probably somewhere around here if you want to look," Starlight shrugged.

"Really?"

"Yeah. Oh- here we are!" A gigantic building had appeared out of the mist. The path led to a set of huge doors with what was supposedly the IDTA logo or crest on them. As they drew closer, Gil could see what looked like a speaker to the left of the doors. A tiny blue light was blinking on its right side and as Starlight approached it, a blue plane of light appeared and scanned over her body.

"Star of Atlantis, Welcome to IDTA." The voice was male and you could hear the amusement in the robotic prose as the massive doors slid open and light poured out.

"Hey Larry. How ya been?"

"Been fine, thanks for asking. I assume this large population is the majority of the R&R?"

"Yes, hang on." She turned to address the crowd, floating a foot above their heads so they could all see her. "Alright ladies and gentlemen, people of all ages- listen up, cause I'm only gonna say this once! This is IDTA, the Inter-Dimensional Traveling Agency. Basically the new R&R but way cooler. So if you want in, that's great! We're going up against the Darkist, and for anyone who decides it's not for them- that's fine. No one has any obligations to stay here and you can leave at any time you want, but I'm warning you," she paused and surveyed the crowd. "If you do decide you don't want to be here, your only options are to try the City or go back to the land of the living and try again. If you choose the second option, you will have no memory of this place or what happened here. If you try the City and you can't get in, you can either give up and go to the Hole- which is a terrible place by the way- or come back here. We may or may not take you back, depends on your reason for leaving. If you get kicked out, we won't take you back."

She came to a stop and caught her breath before finishing with. "There are rules, you will follow them, but everywhere has rules. That being said, the main reason IDTA is here is to have fun. That's also rule number one! As you enter, Larry will scan you and you can follow the blue lines to your new rooms. Dinner is in an hour and training begins tomorrow. There is no curfew as the walls are all sound proof. If you have any questions just ask Larry, he knows almost everything... So, have at it!" Starlight dropped to the ground and stepped aside as people started to get in line for the door.

"Nice speech." Jake grinned and clapped her on the back. "Did you practice it or come up with it on the spot?"

The redhead rolled her eyes and turned back to the line. Names were being declared as people stepped forward one at a time to walk through to doors. Some reactions were actually quite funny as some people didn't know their real names while others didn't want anyone else to know. As soon as Scott stepped forwards Gil grinned and called out, "Why'd you die on me? Wait for me inside dude!"

Scott nodded and waved as he stepped through. Other names that they knew came up and soon almost everyone was inside, leaving only Starlight, Jake, Robert, and a small group still in line. The last person to step through bought the inventor's attention. "Rose Flyer."

"Rose? Rose!" he ran to her, grinning like a fool. "I thought you were dead!"

"Well you thought wrong. I'm alive, so far. Luna here- well Starlight, we met when I was five and grew up together. She asked us to be her new parents for the next cycle and we agreed, did you know that she could time travel?"

"No I did not." The two men said in unison before looking at each other and laughing.

"Well, she does. I met one version of her that was trying to catch up to her original time stream and she asked us to take care of her as a baby- the one in the correct time steam. Or at least that's how you explained it." Rose looked at the Blender.

"Yeah something like that. Anyway, it didn't work out so I made sure Rose didn't get killed in the Darkist invasion of Four and brought her to R&R. She's been there ever since." Starlight waved her hand dismissively. "Why don't we all go inside and talk there?"

"Good idea. Training does start tomorrow after all," Jake grinned. "Good to see you Rose."

"Same. I hope you boys have been alright," she followed Starlight as the Blender led the way into the building. As soon as they stepped inside, Starlight was attacked by a small floating blur that zipped around her ticking furiously. She laughed, bent down, and opened her arms as the blur slowed down and huddled in her embrace. "I missed you too little guy." She turned to her friends, "You remember Tokemi right?"

"Yeah! Hey squirt!" Robert grinned, bending down to rub the little Time Demon's head. "How've you been?" Tokemi ticked happily and went to each person, gathering affection.

"Larry?" Starlight asked as she stood up.

"Yes?" the voice seemed to come from everywhere at once.

"How's that Holo-me working for you?"

"It's great." Heads whipped around as the voice came from a set location. Leaning against the wall with his arms crossed was a teal haired young man in a suit comprised of various blue tones. The skin that was visible was a porcelain color. He had thin light blue tattooed lines along his high cheekbones, a pair of goggles sat on his head and had diamond shaped earrings made of Portal Crystals dangling from his ears. Nestled in the right one was an intimidating earpiece. His eyes were a glowing neon light blueish-teal color and were focused on Starlight.

She laughed at the smug smirk on the AI's face and rolled her eyes. "Perfect. How's everything running?"

"There's been a few bugs here and there, but the overall performance is doing surprisingly well for such a large system," he replied, joining their group which had resumed walking -or bouncing in Tokemi's case. "Would you like me to give the tour?"

Starlight tilted her head. "You guys wanna hang in your rooms until dinner or..."

"We'll take the tour." Robert laughed. "So... Luna..."

"Yeah... I use it as my innocent little kid name," the redhead shrugged. "So straight ahead is the Common Room. I guess it's like a multipurpose room really, but it's in a central location. That's where dinner will be." She pointed to her left saying, "That's the East Wing. It's for the newcomers and trainees. But since that's everyone right now, we're not using it for living quarters. I'll go over all the important stuff at dinner. On your right is the West Wing. Not very original I grant you, but it serves its purpose. That's for the officers. And towards the back on the other side of the Common Room is the members' area, the North Wing. The upper floors are for the leaders and founders. Again I haven't worked out the details for all that, but this is a democracy people- that's what voting is for!"

They entered through the big open doorway and into the Common Room. The place was enormous. The ceiling was three stories high and the bare floor the size of a stadium. "For now, I've just assigned everyone a room in the North Wing. But I do need a command group and I'd like you guys to be a part." Starlight looked at her reunited family and smiled.

"Yeah sure." Jake grinned. "Look at you. Head of a new organization! That's my girl!"

"Thanks Jake," she rolled her eyes and grinned, giving him a hug.

"So what's all this about time travel?" Robert asked.

She explained the whole situation in full while Larry continued the tour. By the time they had explored the whole bottom floor it was time for dinner. Blue lights had appeared on the floors all traveling in the direction of the Common Room. The empty floor had been supplied with ten long tables near the center with a bunch of smaller tables surrounding them. Each place setting was complete with plate, silverware, cup, napkin and an electronic pad and stylus. People had already started sitting down and were looking around for any sign of food. Starlight led her companions over to the largest of the small tables and was soon joined by the rest of their friends. Starlight was still wearing the earpiece from R&R and had hooked it up to the IDTA sound system. Her voice, coming in through the speakers, quickly grabbed everyone's attention.

"Okay, so this is how food here works. As you are all the first residents, permanent or otherwise, there is no menu yet. I was in a bit of a hurry, so I didn't program anything in. Just write what you want to eat on the pad at your place setting and it should appear on your plate. This is the first time I've tried this so please try to be thorough in your description. To send the order just tap the button near the top."

She sat down and turned to her friends. "This is where that Soulforce reader thing comes in handy. Memories are stored in two places," she explained. "Your brain, and your soul. So the Soulforce reader can scan the memory you're thinking of and send it to the computer."

"Which is what *really* orders the food," Katie surmised. "Writing it on the pad makes them think of it. Then the button activates the reader. Smart."

"Like I said, it's a first try for this."

"But what about the food?" Robert asked as their table began trying it out.

"Food made to order like this isn't my invention," Starlight grinned. "It's been done before."

"Who makes it?" he clarified.

"Larry does."

"But how?"

Starlight rolled her eyes as if the answer was self-evident. "Portal Crystal energy. That's usually going to be the answer around here. If you want to watch it in action, go to the kitchens. You know where they are now. It just looks like blue energy swirling around the food and everything kinda goes too fast to see unless you record it and play it in slow-mo."

"Well," Lester interrupted. "That sound fascinating, but I'm hungry. How long does it take?"

"How much did you order?" Arya countered. "Oh, Starlight, I forgot to ask. What happened to Ben?"

"He's over there." The redhead pointed to one of the outlying tables where the elf was sitting alone.

"You're letting him just walk around?" Jake asked incredulously.

"It's not like he can go anywhere or do anything he's not supposed to." Starlight shrugged. "Everything here is Soulforce coded and locked. So even if someone could change his DNA," she looked pointedly at Gil. "It wouldn't help. IDTA is a good place for second chances. And I'm making sure Ben gets his. He was only trying save your planet, Arya."

She nodded and looked down. Most of them had gotten their food by now and were eating silently, watching the exchange. Lester's plate was piled high with all sorts of food.

"That brings me to the subject of command." Starlight said setting down her fork.

"How does-" Dare started to ask but the Blender forged ahead.

"We need to come up with a command system. Well, no, we need to decide who's part of it. I already have something in mind."

"Like what?" Arya asked.

"Highest rank is the Founders. I've decided there's only three of those, so there's a tie breaker. Next is Leaders, there's nine of those. Then Officers... depending on how many Members there are, I'd say probably about a one to eight ratio there. Then Members- those slots are always open. And lastly Trainees- the new people. Everyone here is technically a Trainee but we're a little starved for recruits so..."

"Right. And who's going to be on the higher up levels?"

"Well... everyone gets a say about how things are done, so we'll let them decide. You'll all get to vote too." she winked. "For now though, I'm going to say that we're Leaders. Since I built this place from scratch I think I should be a Founder."

"Hey, we all get to decide if you are or not! But..." Dare grinned. "I suppose it is fair. After all, I'm supposed to be dead right now."

"You *are* dead right now. This particular place admits both dead and alive." Starlight laughed at his affronted expression. "We'll work out the specifics tomorrow. I'm going to bed. See ya." She stood from the table and remains of her food dematerialized. She met Larry, who hadn't gone to eat with them, outside with Tokemi hot on her heels. "So that thing we were working on... is it done yet?"

"Almost. The final coding should be done by tomorrow morning," he said as she started walking for her room. Unlike everyone else, she had made a personalized room on one of the top floors. Perks of building the place. She took the elevator up and entered the floor. It was coded to her Soulforce and currently, no one else could get in. *I'll have to change that*, she thought. Quickly getting ready for bed, the Blender said goodnight to Larry, slipped into bed, and turned off the lights. Tomorrow was going to be interesting.

CHAPTER 28

The next morning was busy. People were getting up to have breakfast and being assigned to teams for training. Once everyone had gathered in the Common Room and were mostly done eating, Starlight stood up. "First things first," she addressed the crowd. "We need some kind of command to be set up. Everyone gets a say, but only one say. Cast your vote by writing your choices on you pad." She went on to explain the situation and recommended people with the most experience, including those not inside her direct group of friends.

It was silent as people voted, and once everyone had finished Larry, who was using his Holo-me, announced the selected names. "Founders are Star of Atlantis, Arya Greylance, and Jake Gilgalad. Leaders are Robert Gilgalad, Gillian, Katie Boardo, Scott Aster, Lester Greylance, Loki, Rose Flyer, Alastor Azazel, and Leaf Ataray." He went on to give all the officers. In total there were about 4000 members and 500 officers.

All of the officers had been trained in various styles of fighting and most in first aid. Arya had decided that everyone should at least know the basics in hand to hand combat as well as weapons training, so everyone reported to their officer and broke off into their teams. Starlight had grabbed her friends and they had gone to the upper levels. The second floor had a lot of advanced training features and the Sims.

Short for Simulation, the Sims were virtual realities created and maintained by Larry. "I'll show you how they work later." Starlight said as they passed by the rooms. She led them to the armory and let them look around. "See, told you. Way more advanced than R&R's stuff," she told Gil.

"I can see that. No wonder you just left it all for the Darkist. Compared to this, those weapons are *ages* behind." He picked up a gun with glowing blue lines on it. "What's-"

"Portal Crystal energy."

"But-"

"Just go with it. Larry and I have worked on containing the energy. Oh! I almost forgot to show you! Our Portal."

"Portal?" Katie blurted out. "You know the-"

"Relax. Everything is Soulforce coded remember. Nothing goes through unless I say so. Plus this particular Portal is special. You know how regular Portals use a fraction of a Crystal to power it? This one uses whole Crystals- plural. All in all there's about fifty Crystals powering this thing. It uses the raw energy, no converters. *And...* It can send stuff through Time as well as space." The Blender said proudly. "Technically there's no time in this dimension, our minds just process things as normal. We're outside of Time so if we go anywhere else, we reenter Time."

"So the Portal has to be able to send people to all times." Robert concluded.

"Exactly. It's on the first floor though. We can check it out later. Only officers and up can use it and only if they have special clearance." She led the group through the floor pointing out the notable features. On the next floor up was the Leader's quarters. Each got their own suite and there was a central common room with a small kitchen and lounge. The floor above that was the Founders'. It was set up the same, but with more space as there were less of them. On the highest floor was the Control Center.

As everyone claimed their rooms Starlight explained how they could ask Larry to personalize their rooms. "Honestly, I already claimed my room when I was building IDTA so everything is already there. You can all come see if you want an example."

She led the party up to her room and fixed the settings so they all had access. It was an impressive example of creative personalization. She had a water feature in one corner, complete with water slide and rope swing. Her bed was located in a treehouse up by the ceiling accessed by a rock wall or rope bridge leading from a platform in the other corner. Tokemi, asleep in the reading nook located in the final corner, rolled over and snuggled deeper into the nest of pillows.

Her walls were painted to look like nature scenes- each wall had something different. One was a beach with rolling waves, one a summer forest with sunlight filtering through the leaves, one a mountain range, and one an underwater landscape. But they were all *moving*. The waves crashed into the shore, leaves flowed in the breeze, clouds billowed across the sky, and the seaweed danced in the current; but there was no sound. Everything was completely silent. The ceiling reflected the time of day and the sun, the only light source in the room, was slowly but steadily climbing higher. At night the moon provided enough light to read by. Dominating the floor, was rich dark green carpet, reminiscent of grass.

As everyone was marveling at the room, Starlight opened the closet and grinned. "I may just happen to have a personal Sim room in here..."

"Seems like you thought of everything." Rose praised.

"But what about the food?" Lester groaned.

"There's a fully stocked kitchen in the floor's common room." Starlight laughed. "So everyone get the idea? You can literally have anything in your room, so long as it fits."

"That is best thing ever!" the elf laughed.

The redheaded Blender quickly agreed and led the group up to the top floor. They walked up the final flight of stairs which set them in the center of the circular room. Smaller than all the others, but still big, the Control Room was stuffed full of computers, buttons, and monitors of all kinds. There were slanted windows all around giving a lovely view of the surrounding mist. The nearest patches had a blue tinge to them, but the mist was so thick that it completely covered the Portal Crystals' glow.

"Welcome to my room." Larry's voice came from everywhere and the room was suddenly lit up. The walls were the same soft white color that furnished the rest of the room. The blue theme continued here- the signature glowing bits were on most every surface, but the overall effect wasn't overpowering. Rather, it gave a feeling of mystery to the complex.

"Hey Larry. Okay guys, since most of us know how to accomplish the things everyone else is practicing down stairs, I thought we could figure out what to do about a certain problem." She fixed everyone with a serious stare. "Admittedly, this problem is mostly mine, and not to exaggerate on my own importance, but if I can't deal with it, you're all royally screwed."

She went on to explain about Sanyia and the deal she had made. Loki added in his part in the operation, explaining how the Blender had asked him to follow Joshua around. Starlight wrapped up the narrative by saying, "So if we can't get Joshua to throw away his immortality or at least release Saniya, then I get stuck in a Time loop and your jobs will be infinitely harder. With Sanyia under Joshua's command, the Darkist can't lose." Her gaze was caught by movement on the stairs. A sleepy Tokemi emerged and made his way to her feet, latching onto her leg and ticking fast enough to cause a purr.

"Luckily we have Tokemi here, who can do the same things as Saniya, although I've never actually seen him do anything Time related." She grinned at the little floating demon.

"So we need to get Joshua to release Saniya," Arya verified.

"I don't think Saniya actually cares if Joshua is immortal or not, just so long as the demon is free eventually- if Joshua dies of old age or just decides to release Sanyia. The demon is under contract not to harm or cause Joshua's death; and as he's immortal right now he physically can't die which is why we need him to be mortal again so Sanyia will be released."

"So how do we do that?" Gil asked.

"Um… We have a onetime chance. In two days Joshua will be able to make his choice and hopefully we can convince him to choose mortality again. Otherwise I- *we* are stuck." Starlight sat down in one of the chairs and glanced at the screen.

Larry's voice suddenly spoke up. "The thing you asked about is done now. We can try it out whenever you're ready."

The redheaded Blender perked up and grinned. "Yeah, we can do it now. Gil, this is also for you if you want it. We're pretty much done here now, everyone just think of some good convincing lines and we'll see if it works. I'll tell you the details of where and when later. I've been waiting for this!"

"Waiting for *what*?" Gil asked pointedly.

Starlight smiled and the hope on her face was clear. "Larry and I have come up with a way to contain my memories. You know how I have so many that I can't process them? That's why I do the whole adoption thing- so I can forget them and they won't drive me crazy. Ever since Gil found me in that cave, I've been having flashbacks and dreams and it's annoying the heck out of me!"

"What do you mean 'contain' them?" the green haired male asked.

"I mean exactly that. We figured out a way to get them out of my head and onto some of Larry's servers. And I mean literally out of my head- I won't have access to them unless I specifically ask Larry for them. Or I look it up on a computer."

"So you mean you'll be able to just pull up videos of your entire life?" Scott grinned. "Wish I could do that! All those times I did a sweet move and nobody saw it? I wish!"

"We'll see what we can do, but my memories will most likely take up all the available space," she laughed. "Larry, where's it set up?"

"Seeing as this is a test run, the infirmary. Just in case."

"Good thinking. How long do you think it's going to take?"

"No idea, but I'd expect it'll take a while."

Starlight nodded and looked at her friends. "Well, you heard him. This is gonna be a while. You guys can do whatever you want. Larry, show them the Sims will ya?" She smiled excitedly then raced down the stairs. Tokemi, who had been flung off her leg when she started forward, was picked up by Robert. He and Gil followed the redhead down to the infirmary on the first floor.

Connecting the trainee and member's wings, the infirmary was a long room filled with all sorts of medical aids and appliances. Rows of sick beds lined the wall separated by curtains giving the appearance of an emergency room. Separated by a glass wall, the operating suite resided directly to the left of the doors for easy access. Larry was standing by the nearest sick bed with an interesting and slightly intimidating contraption.

Starlight moved forward, followed by Robert, while Gil dragged a seat over to the bed. As the redhead got settled on the bed, Larry attached the wires to her. She grinned at Robert. "What does this remind you of?"

The inventor shook his head, laughing. "Don't even go there. Think we'll get to see you alters?"

"Probably not." She turned to the teal haired AI. "So how does this work?"

"It will probably take some effort on your part, but the computer will do most of the work. No one's ever done this before, so I can't tell you what to expect, but you'll probably have to-" His voice was cut off as he switched on the machine. Starlight closed her eyes to the faces of her slightly worried friends. When she opened them she was in familiar settings.

The walls of her old bedroom greeted her, but this time only Trouble was waiting for her. "Where are the others?"

"In their rooms," Trouble shrugged. She was lying on the bed reading and had put the book down as Starlight came in.

"Why aren't you?"

"Someone has to watch the screen." She closed her book and hopped off the bed. "So what's up?"

"Haven't you been watching the screen?" Starlight grinned. "We're cleaning house."

"You mean Larry finished the memory thing?"

"Yup. So how are we supposed to do this?"

"Looks like we're going to have to enter the depths of your mind!" the alter said dramatically. "But we're seriously going to need some way to get unlost if the worst happens."

"Not going to be a problem. While you all have been napping, I've been practicing coming in here. I've got most of the maze mapped out, or at least all the major hallways. There are lights in those ones and arrows pointing back here. We can start with the nearest stuff and make our way in, but I'm going to need everyone's help."

"Sure thing. ALTERS! FALL IN!" she yelled. The sound of doors slamming and running steps could be heard as the others made their way out. They formed a line across the room and turned to face Trouble. "We're cleaning house!" she informed them. "All of it goes. Star, you have the link?"

The purpose of the various wires attached to her body was to gather the memories and transport them to Larry's servers. Starlight felt for the link to the wires and firmly grasped it before nodding to her main alter. "Locked in and ready."

"Good. Luna, Mari- I want you two to stay here and throw the memories out through the doors. Simon, Jordan- you're in charge of the outer limits. After we clear that out, make a chain and carry the inner memories to the kids. Anna, Chase- you get the inner. Starlight and I will take the core."

"What about me?" Ivy's voice was like melted steel.

"We don't trust you. Stay in your room." Trouble glared at her.

"And what if I don't?"

"Then we'll lock you in," Chase said firmly.

"All I'm staying is that getting rid of the memories will benefit me. Why would I mess this up?"

The others shared a look and Anna spoke up. "You may get rid of memories that Star needs to keep."

Ivy looked as if she was about to snap out some retort, but wisely kept her mouth shut. She acquiesced and made her way back to her room followed by Chase, who closed the bedroom door after her and turned the key. The door locked with a satisfying click. The alters grinned and ran off to their assigned jobs.

"Don't throw anything out unless I say it can go. I'll tag it." Starlight told the younger girls before they ran off.

"Well..." Trouble grinned. "Shall we start?"

CHAPTER 29

They had been at it for several weeks, although out in the real world it was only a few hours, and they hadn't even made it past the outer corridors. Everyone was working as fast as they could, literally shoveling the memories out to the next person, who passed it to the next person, who passed it to the girls, who shoved them out the doors where they made their way through the wires to Larry's servers. It was quite a process.

"What about this one?" Simon asked holding up the memory. The memories looked like glowing cubes in various colors, and were stacked next to and on top of each other, taking up all available space in each room. No, *room* implies a certain limitation; the spaces the memories were residing in could only be described as massive halls, the ceilings of which were lost to sight in the shadows. Starlight and the alters had cleared five hundred and twenty seven of them. They worked fast.

Starlight examined the memory Simon was holding up, glimpses of what it contained flashed across the surface. The alters knew what type of memory to keep and which ones to throw out, but for any unsure cases they referred to her. "Toss it," she said, going back to her own patch.

"How many more rooms are there?" Jordan groaned.

"Probably about a billion more than what we've already done." Starlight shrugged. "Don't you have access to them?"

"Yeah but I never felt like getting lost in here." The rebel replied.

"Good point. Come on people, keep at it!" The false enthusiasm in her voice was almost a tangible thing. "We've only got one billion more rooms to go."

She picked up another memory and saw something that caught her attention so she flipped the top open and took a look at the contents.

She was flying over a forested area when a cry for help drew her attention. Landing silently among the dense foliage she peered out from behind a tree and watched the drama unfold before her. A girl, dressed in rather expensive clothing, was glaring up at a blonde haired young man. Arms crossed and eyes blazing, she continued to brazenly call for help while dropping expletives that would make even Captain Azazel blink. Her companion just stood and stared open mouthed. After a while, her cries still waiting to be answered, she stomped her foot and shoved the man back. Caught off guard, he stumbled, fell, and abruptly sat down hard. His eyes never left hers. She cursed at him and stomped off into the wood.

Starlight grinned and took the opportunity presented to her. She stepped out from behind the tree and helped the man up. He was so startled by the girl's actions that he didn't notice Starlight until she was gripping his hand and pulling him to his feet. Staring at her, he blinked then broke into a huge grin.

"Saw the whole thing?" he asked.

"Yup, and I gotta say- what'd you do to piss her off like that?"

"Unreturned love. But then she's in love with practically everyone so no surprise there. All the other fellows bend over backwards for her, the spoiled brat."

"I see. Star."

"Loki." The two shook hands.

Starlight closed the memory and smiled setting it in the 'keep' pile, then reached for another one.

✪ ✪ ✪

Katie ducked the rapid fire, rolling into cover under a fallen spaceship. The sky was dotted with aircraft from both sides. The noise was deafening even through her sealed helmet. She grabbed the bottle of healing tonic off her belt and took a swig. Her injured leg was instantly good as new and she sighed in relief. She started to scan her surroundings, then the world went black.

Annoyed, Katie stood up as words flashed across her vision. "Game over. Player-4 killed by Player-7." The Sim room pixelated back into existence and she stepped off her pad. Only two of the original eleven people were still playing- Dare and Arya were going head to head in the points department and were currently running around the city looking for each other. In less than sixty seconds the final death match would start and they'd both be teleported to the city's center. Katie joined the 'dead' players in front of the master game screen. "You did way better than last time," Gil grinned.

"I beat *you* by miles!" she retorted.

"Hey that explosion came outta nowhere!" he protested.

"I thought Blenders couldn't die."

"In real life yeah, but in a PVP Sim?" he shook his head dramatically. "I'm just as breakable as everyone else. Dare or Arya?"

"I'm going for Arya. You?"

"Dare. How much longer do you think Starlight is going to be?" he asked, brushing the bright green hair out of his eyes.

"Robert says she's about a third of the way done. At this rate she should be done by tomorrow afternoon."

"That's good. I asked Loki and he said that Joshua's choice is the day after tomorrow. How's the plan for that going?"

"Well, without Star it's hard. She's the only one that knows all the specifics about it. Loki only knows *when* it's happening not where."

"And the Members?"

"Rapidly becoming elite warriors, but don't we technically not have time here? We can just pop up at the right time and place for the show."

"Starlight said something about that- she likes to stick to the 'Master Time' as she called it. The one all the other portals are linked to. Apparently it was a condition to set up shop here."

"That's all well and good, but there *is* no time here," Gil said. "How are we supposed to go with the flow when there's no flow?"

"That's just what she said, okay? I don't know-" she was interrupted by Loki.

"Just ask her when she gets out of her mind meld." The trickster shrugged.

"What?"

"It's an earth thing."

Katie rolled her eyes and turned back to the screen. "I'll bet it is," she muttered.

✪ ✪ ✪

Dare slammed into the wall, breathing hard. Not only did he have to off Arya to win, hordes of mixed enemies were also attacking. It was every man for himself now and his main opponent was nowhere to be found. The final death match had started a few minutes ago and the rest of his team was probably watching his progress on the screen. Time was flowing faster inside the game than outside, so his actions probably look accelerated to them.

He shook his healing bottle- empty. *Just peachy*, he thought. He thought back to when Larry had first shown them the Sims. The AI had started some kind of instructional Sim for them before letting them try out the real thing. This was Dare's seventh Sim now, not including the tutorial one, and he had to agree with the computer- they were definitely good for training. *And one of the best recreational activities ever created*, he added silently.

He suddenly caught a glimpse of his target. Arya was standing out in the open waiting for him. "Finally." He left the safety of his wall and walked out to meet her. "Seen any of those annoying pricks lately?"

"Killed the last one, hopefully. How you liking this setting?" She gestured to the post-apocalyptic city around them.

"IDTA's cooler."

"Heck yeah. But think about setting up a clu-" she struck mid-sentence, but Dare was ready for her. In absence of his gun, he had drawn his knife and the ring of steel on steel signaled the start of some epic background music. They both laughed at Larry's choice of music and resumed fighting. The atmosphere was loose and relaxed as the two actually discussed the weather while 'locked in epic battle'. True, the voice narrating their actions was distracting, but they managed to block it out.

After several swings and a roll, Dare had Arya pinned to the ground. "Well this is awkward," she grinned and reversed the hold.

Dare looked up at Arya and laughed. "And this is better?"

"Much." She smirked and drove her knife into his chest. The world instantly got dark and the two exited the game as the stats played. Stepping off their pads, Dare walked over and they shook hands.

"Good game."

"Told you I'd get you back for last time." She winked and they turned to their friends. Money was exchanging hands and congratulations were being offered.

"What happened Dare?" Scott grinned, drawing the ex-guard into his embrace. "You had her!"

"Dude, you told me to let her win!" Dare shook his head laughing. "What was I supposed to do? You didn't bet on me did you?"

"No, and I doubt you let her win. Apparently you're equally matched, if the last few games have been any indication." He turned and addressed the group, "Anyone up for a good old fashioned racing game?"

"After lunch!" Lester said. "Besides we should check on the Member's progress."

"You're just always hungry." Arya punched his shoulder.

"Ow! So? It's still lunch time," the elf pouted. He took Katie's hand and pulled her out of the room.

"So are those two officially dating or..."

"Shut up Gil." Arya punched him.

"Ow. Well, let's go then. I'm in the mood for blueberry muffins." The Blender grinned.

"What are blueberries?"

"It's an earth thing." He and Jake said simultaneously.

Several hours later the Common room was filled with people and the sounds of laughter and music. Colored lights flashed as people danced or socialized. Every member was there with the exception of the two Blenders. Starlight was still clearing out her head, and Gil was babysitting. Truth be told he wanted to be there when she woke up. There was only one memory thing and as soon as she was done, he wanted his turn.

Gil had met one other Blender besides Starlight but he or she, Gil have never discovered their original gender, was the youngest of the three of them. Starlight was the oldest and had the most memories. To his knowledge, the other Blender had never messed with time and neither had he for that matter. Only Starlight and the Time Beings had successfully traveled through Time. Anything else wasn't true Time travel. The way his father had described it to him, it wasn't possible. He thought back, remembering the speech.

When he had asked his father if he could go back and save his mother, the man had sat him down and looked him in the eye.

"Let's say that you all of a sudden get this crazy idea into your head that time travel is a good idea, (which it really isn't but whatever) and you travel back in time to... whenever," he began. "Let's call the place you started out Home. Home is essentially the exact moment in time that you exist. If you leave it, you enter another dimension. Whether you're time traveling or just going to a completely different dimension, you have left Home.

"When you travel backwards or forwards in time you enter a different time stream. IT'S NOT THE SAME DIMENSION AS HOME! It may look like it is, but no matter what you do in that place, the events in Home NEVER CHANGE. Home is the exact point in time that you left and it's not possible to

travel back in time at Home. You're already traveling into the future at the normal pace of seconds, minutes, hours, etc.

"So, if you travel back in time and kill your grandfather, nothing happens to you because you're not actually from that time and YOU CANNOT CHANGE HOME! When you travel, you create a new dimension, a copy of Home. It's only a copy, and no matter what you do there, HOME DOES NOT CHANGE! You can make as many copies as you want, literally an infinite amount- as you can make copies of the copies and alternate realities of the copies you made of the copies and on and on and on.

"When you leave Home, NO TIME PASSES at Home. When you get back Home, NO TIME HAS PASSED, it's like you never left. Since no time has passed, you haven't aged. You are connected to Home and ONLY THE THINGS YOU DO IN HOME affect your existence.

"Since NO TIME HAS PASSED at Home, you never actually left, but yet you still remember everything that happened while you were gone. This can be confusing because if you make more than one copy of an alternate universe or a different dimension, then you get your facts mixed up, similar to reading a lot of fanfiction then trying to remember the original story without reading it over again. If you make too many copies, then you're in for a serious headache. AVOID MAKING MORE THAN ONE COPY OF SOMETHING!

"YOU AGE ONLY IN HOME!!! The time you spend at Home is the only time you age. This can be a problem if you don't have the ability to make yourself appear older or younger than you actually are like a Blender. You can be infinitely many years old but still only be 15 at Home. You can make a parallel universe of Home, (THAT'S NOT REALLY HOME, THERE IS ONLY ONE HOME) and live until it ends, then go back to Home and say you know the

future. THIS IS NOT TRUE!!! The copy of Home may be similar to Home, but future events in Home are not fixed and depend on your influenced actions.

"That is why traveling is a bad idea," he sighed. "The influence of other dimensions can affect the outcome of Home, BUT ONLY IF YOU LET IT. You need to be able to lock up unneeded memories that could affect Home so nothing drastic happens. If you don't have access to this life saving and required feature, DO NOT ATTEMPT TO TRAVEL! YOU HAVE BEEN WARNED!"

Gil's father sat back and watched his son's reaction. *"That's why going back to save your mother is a wasted effort, son. This rule applies to everyone except Time Beings and trust me, you don't want me to get started on those."*

Gil sighed looking at the only non Time Being ever in existence to actually time travel. He realized now why she did it- why she went through those cycles. Starlight had made way too many copies and has serious mental issues as a result. That's why she wanted Larry to withhold memories of things that have nothing to do with what was happening now. She wanted to lock up her unneeded memories that could affect Home so nothing drastic happened to Home. The only problem was, which Home was *her* Home?

He hoped it was this one. It was all so confusing, so no wonder she was crazy. Just hearing his father's speech had given him a headache. *I'm never going to time travel,* he thought. *Lesson learned.*

CHAPTER 30

Starlight wiped her forehead. She and the alters had cleared out most of the rooms and there were only less than ten left. They had finally found the end to the endless hallways that doubled back crossing space that was already used extending into the Tenth Dimension. The Tenth Dimension, as Starlight called it, was another word for the ΖΣЯΘs or more accurately included the ΖΣЯΘs *and* the Crossroads. As she had explained to the alters, "The Crossroads isn't in the ΖΣЯΘs."

Now only ten doors down, five on each side, was the final wall. The end. They had explored and mapped out every last bit of her mind. Sometimes, in some dusty corner, they'd find a half developed alter hanging around, flittering in and out of existence. Whenever one of these was found, Starlight took pity on them and ended their pitiful existence. Standing in front of the final wall however, was something different.

It looked like an alter, but was entirely blue in color. Portal Crystal blue. But it's eyes were glowing white. It had no definite gender and was just standing there staring blankly ahead. "What is it?" Trouble asked.

"I dunno. You guys keep working, I'll go check it out." Starlight frowned and walked right up to the figure without getting a reaction. She waved her hand in front of its face and stared fixedly at it. When she had moved her hand, so had it, in the exact same motion. She grinned and decided to act like a moron, jumping up and down and waving her arms. It did the same. "Hey Trouble! Come check this out!"

Her main alter came up behind her and frowned. "What are you doing?"

"Look." She waved at the figure and it waved back. "See. You try." She stepped back and let Trouble take her place in front of it. Trouble waved experimentally, but nothing happened. She jumped a few times then stepped back.

"I think it only responds to you. Try talking to it."

"Okay... Hi. My name is Starlight."

"My name is Starlight." It echoed.

"Perfect." The Blender looked at her alter. "It just copies me." Trouble just shrugged and went back to work. Starlight tried again. "What are you?"

"You."

The redhead frowned and continued. "You're me?"

"Yes." With an actual response this time, Starlight started to take it more seriously.

"Why are you glowing?"

"I am your energy self. This is what you are without a body if you use your full potential."

Starlight nodded, humoring the figure. "And I suppose you want me to use my so called full potential?"

"No. That would be the worst thing you could do."

"Wait what? Why?"

"You would cause the end of the ZΣЯΘs. And complete Joshua Flame's goal. To destroy the ZΣЯΘs."

"So you're saying that if I go supernova I'll destroy the *entire* ZΣЯΘs?"

"With the other Blenders, yes."

"How many others are there?"

"Four total. There's a prophecy that all Blenders know."

"Get to the point," the redhead ground out.

"The exact words that were written down somewhere are lost, but the basic idea is that there can only ever be four Blenders and they will determine the fate of the ΖΣЯѲs. Good versus evil and all that. Don't ask me, I don't know anything about it. It's in one of the memories you threw out. Only a mention of it, not the actual prophecy."

"So... I should look into this eventually shouldn't I?"

"Probably."

"Great. Just great." Starlight sighed. "So why are you back here anyway?"

"I'm your beginning and your end. If you've noticed these hallways are arranged in one intricately massive unfinished loop. Your first memory starts here. This is also where your last memory will be."

"But Blenders can't die. I've tried *EVERYTHING*." Her voice broke. "Nothing works. Don't get me wrong, I'm not suicidal, I'm just *tired*. So tired."

"You're right, Blenders can't die. Nothing can kill them."

"Then-"

"But apparently there *is* an end. Don't ask me, I only know what you know."

"I've never- oh never mind." She wiped the tears from her eyes and adjusted her expression. "Well, it looks like we're almost done here, and that means we have to deal with our little immortal problem. Any ideas?"

"I think you know what you're going to do." The figure said.

Starlight nodded and walked back to the room the other alters were clearing. "You guys kept the memories I asked about right?"

"Yeah, still don't know why you want to keep *those* ones. If I were you, which I am, those would be the first to go." Trouble shook her head.

"Yeah well, I've got a plan for them."

"Joshua?"

"Joshua."

⭐ ⭐ ⭐

Erak glanced at his number two. The commander had been increasingly fidgety ever since the battle. He would stay holed up in his room as much as possible and only came out to give orders or work on necessary planning. He was currently hunched over some stats staring into space. "You okay?"

"Fine." He replied shortly.

"You've been acting strange lately. More so than usual."

"I'm fine. I'm working."

"No, you're not. Look, why don't you go get some rest. You look terrible." Erak offered. He almost never let anyone take extra leave, so the offer should have Joshua questioning his sanity, but the Commander didn't even look up.

Erak sighed at sat down next to him. "If you're worried about the R&R, we'll find them. They must have gone somewhere. Don't worry, Star will show her face eventually."

"It's not that."

"Then what is it? Because you're majorly slacking off here. I'm not trying to provoke a fight either. In the past you've pushed through this kind of thing no matter how tired or sick you were. Your efforts have been outstanding and I confess I rely on you, probably too much. Without your help, I would have just had an ideal with no outcome. You made all this possible, so what's wrong?"

After hearing what Erak had said, the immortal suddenly looked up. "There's something important happening tomorrow and I don't know what to do." His voice was shaking. "Say yes or no. If I say yes, then we win. If I say

say no, then eventually you'll be on your own and there's a big chance we will lose. But I don't want to say yes, and I regret ever saying yes in the first place."

"Then why did you?"

Joshua took a breath, and opened his mouth but no words would come out. He shook his head and shivered. "I can't sleep. I can't dream. I can't eat or drink and most of all I can't think straight." He blurted out, pulling at his hair. "I'm long past insane, and it just keeps getting worse."

"Joshua, you just need to take a break. You've been working too hard."

"NO! No. It won't let me. I can't. It torments me and laughs in my face. I just... can't."

Erak put his hand on the distraught man's shoulder. "Listen. I don't know what's up but I'm sure taking a break and getting things straight in your head will help. I can't have a sloppy Commander on my hands." His attempt to lighten the mood was lost on the immortal. "What about Saniya? Can't it help?"

"Not with this. I'm sure it wants me to say no. It can't be free unless I say no."

"That's what this is about?" Erak's voice rose to a scoff. "This is about Saniya?"

"No- Saniya has nothing to do with it. It's just taking advantage of the situation. You know it's never cared about who wins or what happens. It's a Time Demon for the love of- No. It's not about Saniya."

"Then what is it about?"

"I can't tell you. It won't let me."

"What do you mean 'won't let you'? What is it?" Erak asked in frustration.

"I don't know. But it won't leave me alone. You wouldn't believe me before. Why would you now?"

"I'm still not sure I do. I just know something is wrong. Commander, if this affects our work then you need to tell me. You can't let this fail. Whatever it is, you need to think of what's best for our cause. You said yourself that the only way to fix the ZΣЯΘs is to destroy it first. You said the Portal Crystals would do that and now you want to bail?"

"No." Joshua took a deep breath and closed his eyes. "I just need to deal with this first, or there won't be anything to bail *from*. Our efforts will have been wasted."

"Then you'd better say yes to whatever this is." Erak's patience had run out. "You'd better say yes or so help me I'll-"

"You'll what?" he opened his eyes. "I'm immortal like *her*. I can't die. I'm already going through the worst torture conceivable. What can you do that will make it worse?" He was shouting now, his voice taking on a hysterical note.

"Trust me. I can. You're not the only one making the calls here. In case you haven't forgotten, *I'm* the one in charge."

"In charge of what? A little merry band of revolutionaries? There aren't enough Portal stones in the ZΣЯΘs to do what you want. Don't you realize how massive it is? The *only* thing you can do is rule a tiny fraction of the ZΣЯΘs. You can raze that fraction to the ground but it's only a fraction. *No one* can destroy the whole thing. Not your precious Portal Crystals, not Star, not anything. Maybe I should say no, because this whole damn thing is starting to feel pointless."

"Get. Out." Erak's voice was ice. "Get out *now*."

Joshua stood slowly. "You will regret this."

"No. You will. After all what have I got to lose?"

✪ ✪ ✪

Starlight lifted the last memory and held her breath. All of her alters, with the exception of Ivy, were standing around her. It had a strange lock on it that she'd never seen before. Some of the other memories had been locked up, but not like this. This memory had glowing white, thin, but extremely strong chains wrapped around it and the lock had no key hole. She closed her eyes and reached out carefully.

"You sure you should look at this one." Trouble asked.

"Obviously it's important." She slowly unlocked and opened the memory and the events started to play out in a third person point of view unlike the others which had all been first person.

She was standing at the bottom of a pair of white steps. Her surroundings were blindingly white and there was no color in sight besides herself. She was standing naked, wreathed in white light looking up at something. The light glowed brighter and she nodded as if hearing words. Then a stream of blue light collected at her feet, spiraling up her body and overwhelming the white glow. The light condensed around her, molding to her form. What was left standing was an exact replica of the figure standing guard over the final wall in her mind.

It looked directly at her- straight in the eye, and it's gaze was piercing. Then it smiled, the glow intensified, and it suddenly disappeared.

The memory ended and everyone looked at each other in plain awe.

"Guys…" Starlight's eyes were wide. "I think we just witnessed our creation."

CHAPTER 31

Gil started as the redhead before him suddenly bolted upright. "Hey, Star- you okay?"

"Yeah. Yeah, I'm fine," She said distractedly. "Where is everyone?"

"At the party. You done with... that?"

"Yeah." She took a deep breath and closed her eyes.

"Okay, seriously. What happened?" Gil leaned forward.

"I- It- We- I- I'm not sure." She opened her eyes and brushed her hand through her vibrant hair. "There was this last memory. It tripped me up. When I just remember it, I remember looking at an empty space. But when I went back and looked at it inside my head, it was third person, and I- the memory me- was looking directly at the now me. I swear when it happened there was nothing there! Gil what's-" she broke off and stared at her hands. "Tomorrow is the big day. We have to get Joshua to say no and I don't even know where it's supposed to happen."

"Okay- relax. Just calm down. We'll figure this out."

"How?" she looked at him, her face pleading.

"Well... Is there anyone you can ask about this?" Gil frowned, trying to take things step by step.

"No, there's- actually there is one person we can try." She stared intently into his yellowy-orange eyes. "But I don't know where he'd be. He's been dead along time and-"

"Why don't we ask?" Gil interrupted. "I'm sure the City will have records if he's there, and if not then he's in the Hole right?"

"Or some reincarnation something rather. If that's the case then he could be anywhere."

"Well, we'll start with what we've got. Let's try the City." Gil stood up and extended his hand. Starlight looked at it then at him and took it.

"Thanks."

"No problem. First party in the new clubhouse and we miss it." Gil shook his head. "Just our luck."

"Come on mopey, we're going people hunting." She left the room heading towards the main doors. Gil smiled grimly and grabbed his jacket, shrugging it on before following. He caught up with her just inside the main doors talking to Larry.

"Yeah sure, I'll do that. Be careful." The blue AI said before vanishing, presumably back to the party.

"What'd he want?" Gil asked as the doors opened.

"The time we'd be back."

"What'd you tell him?"

"That we'd be back on time."

"Right... Well, shall we?" He gestured towards the doors.

"Ladies first?"

"Of course."

"Coward."

"No. Gentleman." He grinned and pushed her out the doors. She laughed and pulled him with her, causing him to stumble. "Jerk."

"You started it!" she grinned. They walked in silence after that through the mist, which had seeped back onto the path. The bulk of it however, was held back by the shield. This particular shield was the same one that surrounded IDTA. The plans for the Bubbleshield she had borrowed from Robert all those years ago had proven to be very useful.

"Gil, did I ever tell you about something called a Bubbleshield?"

"You may have mentioned it way back when... Why?"

"Well- this shield," she gestured around them. "Is one."

"What? No way!" Gil exclaimed. "You actually managed to build one? What is it exactly anyway? You were kind of vague on the details."

"A bubble shield is a selectively permeable force field that cannot be destroyed." Starlight said in her best commercial/ announcer voice. "It is controlled by the user's mind and is linked to their DNA and Soulforce- as Blenders' DNA changes frequently. Nothing can get in or out without the consent of the user. And now, with the help of Larry, the user can eat- let's say a poisoned Hamburger- without harm. They simply have to think something along the lines of 'I don't want any harmful or toxic products to pass through the Bubbleshield' and Larry will fill in the blanks and set the shield to the proper setting."

"Another use for the shield is defense/offense. Example: Assuming you are using the shield, if someone fires a bullet at you, you have thousands of different options to pick from. You can allow the bullet to hit the shield and appear on the other side, hit the shield and be angled though it out one of the other sides, be reflected back in the exact path it came from, absorb it and store it for future use, as well as many others."

"Wow. So basically it's a bottled superpower?" Gil grinned.

"Basically," Starlight agreed. The two had reached the Crossroads by now and Gil was looking around.

"Is it just me or is this whole place slightly creepy?" He shook his head and started to the path towards the City. "You coming?"

"Yeah." She blinked and shook her head. "Let's go."

"So what do you think my chances to getting in are? I mean, you've been inside and you're way older than me. More time to make poor choices, eh? But seriously, who would actually want to stay there? IDTA is way better and in my opinion way more fun- Star are you even listening?"

"Hmm? Oh yeah, yeah."

"What did I just say then?" Gil gave her a look.

Starlight then proceeded to reel off everything he had just said within the past five minutes. Gil just rolled his eyes and muttered, "That's just cause you're a Blender and have a perfect memory."

When they got to the City gates, Gil was greeted with the sight of two impressive winged figures watching them approach. One was holding a sword and the other, a book. Starlight walked right up to them and grinned. "Nice to see you two again."

"What is your purpose here?" The sword one asked.

"Just want to know if a certain someone is here. His name is Telmarkin and we need to ask him something." Starlight replied. Her performance was top notch, but Gil could tell she was slightly nervous around them. "It's to save the ZΣЯΘs, kinda important," she laughed, resisting the urge to put her hands behind her back like a naughty child.

The angel with the book flipped through the pages and nodded at the redhead. "The person you seek is within."

"Oh. Good. Um... can we go in and talk to him? Or can you send him out here or..." She came to a stop as a messenger walked up from the other sides of the gates. The messenger swiftly gave her message to the book angel and walked back the way she had come.

The book angel turned to Starlight and said, "Your arrival is expected. Charlemagne will take you to him." He nodded to Charlemagne, who opened the gates and gestured for the visitors to follow.

As they walked through the streets Gil finally blurted out, "Charlemagne? Really? *That's* your name?"

Charlemagne sent a glare in his direction and Gil took the hint. In an attempt to change the subject he asked, "What's your friend's name then?"

"Tyndalius."

"Huh. Okay then. I've never hear that one before. Guess the whole St. Peter deal is an Earth thing." Starlight shot him a look that plainly said *shut up before you say something you'll regret.*

After a few minutes, they were led to a house and shown inside. Charlemagne left them there and went back to his place guarding the gate. "Ah, Starlight!" A man hailed them from the top of the stairs. Starlight recognized Telmarkin but he was much younger. "I figured you'd stop by eventually. You never did ask *where* our immortal's choice is going to take place. I assume it's coming up?"

"Yes. So where is it going to be?" Starlight said impatiently.

"That lovely place outside the gates. I believe you call it the Crossroads?" He had descended the stairs and was standing in front of them.

"It's happening *here*?" Starlight blinked.

"Well, yes. All big decisions happen at a crossroads do they not?" Telmarkin winked.

"But- *Here*?"

"Yes child. Now you may want to go figure out what you're going to do about it if you haven't already. It's taking place tomorrow morning- relatively speaking. Go!" He gave her a nudge towards the door. "My daughter, Hannah, will escort you back to the gates." A young girl came forward and took Starlight by the hand. "Farewell, and good luck."

Starlight quickly thanked him as Hannah dragged her out the door. Gil looked at Telmarkin curiously. "You look like someone I used to know."

"I'm your great, great, great, not so great, great, great, great- probably a lot more greats- grandnephew. Now get out of here before you lose track of that girl!" Telmarkin grinned, shoving the green haired Blender out the door and slamming it behind him. Gil ran after Starlight, her bright red hair easy to distinguish within the crowds of people walking around the street. He waved back at the happy people who smiled at him and followed Hannah to the gate.

"Thank you Hannah." He said as Starlight smiled at her. She turned red and gave a shy smile in his direction before running off. Charlemagne and Tyndalius were waiting for them outside the gates. The two Blenders waved as they passed, looked at each other, and burst out laughing once they were a safe distance away.

"I still hold that IDTA is cooler," Gil wiped the tears from his eyes. "It's nice- perfect rather, too perfect- but I'm still up for adventure."

"Truthfully, that's what I built it for. Not as a last line of defense, not as a place to train, but a place to have fun before you decide to retire." She shrugged.

He had no reply to that and they continue walking in silence. Larry greeted them at the door and asked how it had went.

"Good. Turns out the the big choosing ceremony is taking place here at the Crossroads." Starlight replied. "Is everyone still at the party?"

"About half have gone to their rooms, but it's still in full swing. Want me to call the other Founder and Leaders?"

"No. We'll deal with it in the morning. Just get them up as soon as the 'sun' rises." The 'sun' could be seen through the glass roof of the Common Room and the open courtyard in the center of the building. It was really just a projected video loop to give the illusion that they weren't in some empty place with the absence of a sky. It made the occupants feel more comfortable.

"Roger that. You going to bed?" Larry inquired.

"Yeah. Where's Tokemi?"

"Sleeping in your room."

"Okay. Night you two. See ya in the morning." She gave a two fingered salute and headed to her room.

"I think I'm going to turn in as well." Gil muttered and left Larry alone. The IA frowned for a moment before shaking his head and going back to join the party.

✪ ✪ ✪

The next morning was chaotic. Most of the Members would get up and have breakfast around nine o'clock, but people were up before seven that morning. The Founders and Leader had gathered in one of the Sims rooms, going over the plan for the day. Larry was currently running one of several possible scenarios, allowing them to come up with ideas on the spot. It had been decided that the confrontation party would consist of Starlight, Gil, Loki, and Arya. Everyone else would stay inside and keep watch in case something went wrong. Starlight had told them the Plan as well as Plan B, but no one could come up with a foolproof Plan C.

"Anyone know what time this thing is happening?" Dare asked.

"I can't remember the exact time, but roughly... 9:40ish," the redhead replied absentmindedly. She was standing next to the IDTA sign in the Sim, regarding it thoughtfully. "Should we move this? We don't want him to know we're here."

"Might be a good idea," Gil nodded. "Let's run over the plan again. Oh- What about Saniya? Think it will try anything?"

"Seeing as it wants this just as much as we do, probably not," Loki replied. "Larry, what time is it?"

"9:10." The AI's voice came from everywhere.

Starlight grimace, "We should head out within the next ten minutes."

And so, ten minutes later, Starlight, Gil, Loki and Arya made their way to the Crossroads. The most likely outcome would be that Joshua would eventually end up there, but just in case, Loki and Arya headed to the beginning of the path, at the bottom of the stairs.

Then, they waited.

✪ ✪ ✪

Joshua had informally left the Darkist on a sort of permanent holiday. Erak couldn't run things without him and Joshua knew he would beg him to come back. *Well,* he thought. *Erak can beg all he wants but I'm done! I'm just going to do things my way. Who cares if the Darkist lose.* His mental tone had become bitter. *I've suffered enough for them. Saniya can't cause my death even if I am mortal. There are other ways to extend life. I could just take full advantage of Saniya and change time to my advantage.* He nodded resolutely.

Taking in his surroundings once more, he debated where to go. The Hall of Portals was practically empty and the guards hanging around didn't question his presence. His face was too well known around here. *I'll have to fix that eventually.*

Making a snap decision, he entered the nearest Portal. But the destination wasn't what he was expecting.

CHAPTER 32

Loki jumped as someone suddenly appeared in front of him. He was sitting with Arya on the lowest step facing the void when a boy with white hair and golden eyes suddenly showed up. He was dressed in a brown tank top and cargo pants and seemed to blend into the background. Which was strange, considering there *was* no background to blend into. He face looked to be about twelve or thirteen, he was thin, and shorter than average making his stature that of a six year old. He was staring at Loki with mild confusion.

Loki and Arya both stood to their feet and stared at the boy. Arya opened the communications link and said, "Uh... Star. There's someone here and I don't think its Joshua."

"Arya- this is the Crossroads. Dead people come here all the time!"

"Well, what are we supposed to do with him?"

"I don't know. If he wants to try the City, let him, otherwise you'll probably want to refer him to IDTA."

"Okay." She looked at Loki. The boy was still staring at him. "I'll stay here, you give the kid the tour. Stay with him, in case..."

"Yeah." Loki nodded. "Okay, come on kid. What's your name?"

"Zero." The boy's voice was quiet and Loki had to really pay attention to hear him.

"Well, Zero. Welcome to the Crossroads. I hate to break it to you but you're dead."

"I know. I've been here before."

"Wait- you have?"

"Yes."

"Okay... So you've seen everything already, but I bet you haven't seen IDTA yet. It's new." Loki clapped the boy on the shoulder and the two started walking up the stairs. The boy seemed to cling to Loki's side without touching him. And as they disappeared from view, Arya grinned. Loki had always wanted a little brother. She turned her attention back to the Void and caught sight of her target.

Joshua was looking around, very confused. He saw Arya and his eyes narrowed. "You. What are you doing here?"

"For your information, I live here, thank you very much. Come on. They're waiting for you."

"Who?"

"You'll see. Apparently you have an important choice coming up, and I'd hate for you to miss it." Arya took him by the arm and dragged him up the stairs. He didn't struggle or protest, just calmly tried not to trip. She dumped him in front of Starlight and Gil and stepped back.

"Hi, Joshua. How's it going?" the redhead smiled. "Decided what you want to do yet?"

"Yes."

"And what's that?"

"No. The answer is no."

"Goo- What? *No? Really?* Cause I'd have thought that you would be begging to be mortal by now."

"I was," he admitted. "But I've had a change of heart."

"And why's that?"

"I know that it was Loki who's been bugging me all this time, and that you want me to release Saniya. And the answer is no. I've called in a favor and got a so called 'restraining order'. I've also learned a few things over the years." His eyes flashed purple. "And I'm pretty sure you won't like them."

"So there's nothing we can do to convince you?" Starlight asked shooting Gil a look.

"Nothing."

They had been planning on using Starlight's worst memories of immortality on him, but from the look in his eyes he'd had his fair share and had gotten over it just as she had.

"That's it. This calls for drastic measures!" Starlight unceremoniously grabbed Joshua by his ear and pulled the unfortunate immortal along behind her. She took the path leading to the Hole and catching a glimpse of the destination, Joshua finally attempted to break away. But the Blender had him firmly by the ear and he was forced to keep pace with her or lose it.

"Sanyia!" he shouted. "Sanyia!"

"Saniya can't come. It's rather busy at the moment and we've Sanyia-proofed the whole place." Gil grinned. Earlier that morning, Starlight had sent Tokemi to distract Joshua's Time Demon. So far the plan was a success. Despite his small appearance, Tokemi was actually just as powerful as the other demon and according to Larry, was holding his own just fine.

Starlight stopped at the edge of the Hole, shoved Joshua through the glimmering shield before he could utter another word, and jumped in herself. Gil followed immediately after her, leaving Arya- who couldn't fly back out- guarding the entrance.

Joshua screamed as he fell, flailing his arms and legs. Five feet above the ground Gil caught him, his green feathered wings catching the air and causing powerful drafts that would have flattened the immortal to the ground if Gil hadn't been holding him. He set the Commander down and landed gracefully. Starlight joined them a second later, her wings a carbon copy of Gil's except for the red that matched her hair.

"I thought you had dragon-y wings last time," Gil commented.

"I did. But that was last time, and I was trying not to draw attention to myself."

"Ah, so should we make lots of noise?"

"I don't think that will be necessary." Starlight pointed to several pairs of flying shapes closing in on them.

"Now would be a good time to try out that portable Bubbleshield of yours." Gil said quickly.

Starlight nodded and a shimmering membrane enveloped them holding the hordes at bay. Joshua stared open mouthed at the monsters and nervously eyed the shield, weighing his options should it break. He looked at Starlight and she shrugged. "Say yes and we'll get you out of here. Say no and you can stay here for the rest of your existence. And seeing as you can't die, you'd be in for one hell of a ride."

The immortal glared at her as Gil took him by the waist and lept into the air once more. Starlight followed, holding the shield around them, as Gil flew over the lake and came in for a closer inspection. The dark splotches she had seen last time turned out to be hideous looking debris just floating in a swirling current that circled the lake. The heat was intense and Joshua's face was sweating.

"I'll have Gil drop you in." The redhead's grin was downright creepy and bordering on homicidal mania.

"Channeling a bit of Ivy?" Gil asked, slightly intimidated.

"Probably slightly more than necessary," she admitted. Joshua frowned in confusion at the exchange and tried to fight the sheer terror baring down on him. He kept his face impassive as Gil flew a bit lower, but he couldn't stop the sweat from streaming down his face.

"You're bluffing." Joshua shook his head.

"Look me in the eye and tell me that I am." Her voice held a deadly chill to it and her green eyes, usually shining with amusement, glinted dangerously. She caught his gaze and even through the fear, they held a steely determination.

Joshua clenched his teeth and prepared to be dropped, but Starlight had changed her mind. She sighed and signaled Gil to fly back to shore. Joshua's face held a mixture of smug victory and relief. But the redhead hadn't given up yet.

"I do believe that I'd found a plan C," she commented idly. Gil looked at her. The change of attitude momentarily throwing him off. However she kept silent as they flew upwards towards the entrance. The monsters hovering around them were swept away by the strong air currents she had encountered her first time there. The few that made it past were caught by the shield covering the Hole and cast back down.

The redhead dropped the shield covering them once they were out, but continued to fly straight over the Crossroads and right into the Mist. Gil, who was still carrying the abducted immortal, told Arya to follow and warily flew after her. "Star, didn't we agree that we didn't want him to know we were here?"

"Yes, but there's been a change of plan. Don't worry, I've got it covered."

Gil changed his words to thoughts they carried on the conversation in silence. *What about Saniya?* he asked.

He's not going to give that up, but we can try to talk to him. I've had an idea that should work. In order to release Saniya, he has to say the words, 'I, Joshua Flame, terminate my contract with you and release you from my service.' Dramatic, I know. But all we have to do is get him to say the words and whether or not we can get him mortal or not, Saniya will be satisfied. I asked.

Okay, so how are we going to do that?

They had reached the front doors of the building and landed, their wings disappearing as they entered. Joshua, the new comer, was scanned as per usual and Larry didn't question his presence. In fact, Larry was oddly silent. Gil realized that they didn't want Joshua to know he existed. Starlight led them through the hallways to the infirmary and Gil dumped the immortal on one of the nearest beds.

"You're really not going to like what I'm going to do next, so I'll give you a chance to walk away. Release Saniya and we won't bother you again unless you make us." Starlight said simply.

"No."

"Going once."

Joshua remained silent.

"Going twice... Gone. Gil, looks like you'll have to wait your turn once again."

Gil's head whipped towards the memory modifier thing by the side of the bed. "You think that will work?"

"I know it will work. It worked for me. If we can't get him to give it up, we'll make him forget he ever had it in the first place." She said smugly turning to face their captive. "You sure you don't want to reconsider?"

Joshua looked at them and grinned. "Nope, and I doubt whatever you're going to do will work in the long run."

"See, that's where you're wrong. This thing doesn't just repress memories, it physically takes them out of your head and you can't ever get them back, unless a friend of mine is feeling generous. Larry," she called out. "Can you come in here?"

The AI walked through the door in his Holo-me and greeted the Blenders. "Hey guys, how's it going?"

"We just have this one thing to do, then I believe we're good to go." Starlight laughed, "Hook him up."

Larry complied and Joshua found himself unable to move. He struggled in vain as Larry attached the wires to him flipped the switch. "All set. He's no Blender, so manually extracting the memories will work just fine."

"Thanks, I think I'll do it myself. How much should I leave in?" Starlight traded places with Larry and started opening the virtual files of Joshua's memories on the screen.

"However much you feel inclined to leave."

She grinned and didn't even bother to fight down the urges Ivy was undoubtedly sending her. Gil watched her for a few minutes before going to inform the others of the new developments with Larry in tow.

Several hours later Starlight emerged from the infirmary with an unconscious Joshua floating behind her. The others had all gathered in the Common Room and were curiously eyeing the immortal. "Success?" Loki asked. The white haired boy he had escorted there was clinging to his side, but it seemed like most of them didn't even realize he was there. Starlight could feel some kind of energy coming from the boy that was similar to Arya's so she assumed he was an Illusionator like the elf.

Turning her attention to the group, she replied, "So far. He doesn't remember anything, and as soon as he wakes up, Sanyia will be free. Any ideas where I should drop him?"

"Yeah..." Loki grinned.

⊘ ⊘ ⊘

The man woke up to the sight of a blue sky and water in all directions. He was lying on top of a piece of floating debris and clutching a piece of paper. *What am I doing here?* he thought. *Where is here? Who am I?* Try as he might, no information came to mind. It was if his mind was a blank slate. He looked at the paper in his hand. He read it aloud, testing out the sound of his own voice that he couldn't remember.

"'I, Joshua Flame, terminate my contract with you and release you, Sanyia, from my service.' Who the heck is Saniya? And what kind of name is Joshua Flame?" he scoffed. Deciding that it didn't matter, he turned over the paper. For some reason he was in a terrible mood.

His raft suddenly rocked and he peered into the water to see a huge eel-looking thing swimming below. A few yards off, one of them suddenly burst out of the water reaching astounding heights before falling back down and causing an almighty splash. He read the back of the paper and held on to the raft for dear life as the wave crashed over him.

The words echoed in his head. *Enjoy the shnorkelfooses. What in damnation is a shnorkelfoose?*

CHAPTER 33

Starlight and all of IDTA were taking a holiday. She had decreed, with the unanimous approval of all, that they wouldn't be doing anything that day. People were doing random things, and most of the Sim rooms were being used. Starlight herself surprisingly wasn't in a Sim. Instead she and Loki were just lounging around in her room drawing, or in the case of Loki- being drawn. He was sitting in the nest of pillows and blankets that made up Tokemi's bed while the Time Demon was snuggled next to Starlight who was across the room in a makeshift nest.

The redhead was lying propped up against some pillows and had the sketchbook in her lap. She was currently drawing his hands, holding the book, one finger slotted behind the page he was reading, waiting to flip the page. He was so absorbed in the story that he wasn't even aware that she was drawing him.

Loki was one of those people that didn't like being alone, even if there was no conversation or interaction. He was content just to sit in a corner and read so long as there was someone nearby. He didn't like sleeping alone in his room, and his random visits to other people's rooms was becoming a normal habit. He sighed and shifted into a more comfortable position.

Starlight finished up the drawing and frowned at it. There was something missing. She scrutinized Loki and his surrounding and looked at the picture. She couldn't figure out what it was. Then something next to Loki moved, and she suddenly saw Zero. It was like he had appeared out of nowhere but she then realized he'd been there the whole time, she just hadn't noticed him. "Zero," she said quietly.

The boy looked up at her and blinked. "Yes?" his voice, soft as it was, jolted Loki out of his book. He glanced at the boy and frowned.

"Oh, Zero. I forgot you were there."

"People tend to do that. I don't mind."

"Oh. Okay. You sure you just want to sit here with me?"

The boy nodded then looked at Starlight. She frowned then remembered what she was going to say. "How are you doing that? I didn't even know you were there until you moved and I've been staring directly at you both for over an hour."

"People don't notice me," he shrugged. Curling back up against Loki's side, he resumed reading Loki's book. Loki laughed quietly and returned to his book. His arm was wrapped around the younger boy's small frame and he idly moved his hand to pet the boy's head. Starlight added him to the picture and really had to concentrate to focus on him.

As she was drawing his hair, she noticed that there were two triangle shapes on either side of the top of his head. Either Loki didn't seem to notice them, or the trickster was used to them. They looked almost like tiny cat ears that kids would wear on earth for Halloween and they were the same shade as his hair. Once the picture was finished as put it aside and started drawing an inception picture of Tokemi curled into her side. She included her arm and the pad of paper and the pencil drawing the same picture, getting smaller every time the image was repeated.

She looked up to see Loki staring at her, his book finished. "What are you doing?"

"Drawing. Here." She stood up and gave him the two pictures. She stretched and started towards the door. "I'm hungry. Wanna come get lunch?"

"It's almost dinner."

"Dinner then."

"Sure." He stood up and followed her to the elevator. Zero clung to him as usual. Tokemi was left behind, still seemingly asleep and as the door closed shut he cracked open an eye. Rising up off the pillow he had been on, the little demon disappeared with a pop, his big clock spinning.

Downstairs, Starlight had started eating. All of the big tables were gone, leaving the middle of the Common Room open, but most of the smaller table were still there. People came in and out, but there was no big meal time today. People just came in to eat when they were hungry. The room was mostly empty as Loki sat down next to her.

Halfway through her meal the rest of her friends came in, having just finished a Sim. "Hey Star!" Gil sat down on her other side. "Where you been all day?"

"Being antisocial."

"That's nice- guess what we've been doing!" Before she could answer he continued. "We came up with this new Sim! It's like capture the flag but instead of flags we were using people and they could run around and we had to find them. The terrain was awesome! It was constantly changing and there were traps and stuff all over the place! Plus there were monsters that we had to fight off as well as the other team."

"And what do you call this game?"

"Extreme Capture the Flag."

"Very original," she smirked. She was interrupted by a disturbance at the door. "What's going on?"

Larry was escorting a man in and as soon as he had set his eyes on Katie had had started shouting and ran to meet her. The Leader turned towards him and her eyes got wide. "Dad?! Dad!"

He scooped her into his arms and spun her around in circles. "Oh Katie! I missed you!"

"I missed you too Dad! What are you doing here?"

"Well, I saw the sign outside and thought I'd come to investigate."

"So you died?"

"Yeah, guess I pissed off the Darkist one too many times. What are you doing here?"

"I'm one of the Leaders here, and before you ask- no I'm not dead," she laughed.

"Good, because I've got some news."

"Good or bad?" Lester asked walking up to them.

"Dad, this is Lester. He's my boyfriend."

Lester's eyes had gone wide. "I am? And why'd you say it in front of your dad?!"

"'Cause."

Her dad eyed Lester up and down, seemed to find something he liked, and continued speaking like nothing happened. "Good and bad. Good thing is, Commander Joshua Flame has been declared dead. Bad news- Erak is planning something big. He's about fifty percent done, and is finishing up fast. He's captured himself a Blender and-"

"What did the Blender look like?" Gil interrupted anxiously. He and Starlight had drifted closer to the trio along with the rest of the team.

"I don't know. Never saw him. But Erak did have me building something that would contain a Blender."

"Did you ever finish it?"

"Yes and no. It's done, there's just no power source strong enough for it. Portal Crystals won't cut it."

Starlight and Katie looked at each other. "Yes there is," the redhead said. "*More* Portal Crystals."

"So *that's* why he's been having the Scavengers look for them." Robert shook his head. "Hey, Arnold. Long time no see."

"Robby! You dead or escaped?" Arnold grinned.

"Escaped, what else?" The two friends embraced.

"What's this I hear about Blenders?"

"Erak's planning something with them. I only know of two. The one he's got, and that Atlantis girl."

"'That Atlantis girl' at your service," Starlight bowed with a flourish. "The name is Starlight. And this here, is Gil. He's a Blender too."

Gil waved and Arnold's jaw dropped. "You two had better watch out! Erak will stop at nothing to get his hands on you."

"Apparently. He wants me anyway 'cause I annoy him." She shrugged. "What else is new?"

"Do you know the Blender's name?" Gil asked, his anxiousness returning.

"Matt."

"I know him!" Gil turned to Starlight. "We have to go get him!"

"Gil. Chill. We don't know where he is, if Erak managed to get enough power, or anything about this! We can get him, we just have to-"

"There's no time! He's not like us! He's- he's the youngest so far. I was there when he was born. His mom didn't make it and he never knew his father. He's like family to me."

"How old is he?"

"Only about a hundred of your cycles."

Starlight raised her eyebrows. "That's- he's-"

"For us, about a four year old. But he usually likes to physically be about nine. He's a child in every way and I can't leave him to Erak! He's just a child!"

"Gil." She put her hand on his shoulder and pushed waves of calm into him. "We'll get him. I promise."

❂ ❂ ❂

Erak grinned down at the pathetic figure in front of him. It had taken the guise of a young child, only eight or nine years old and was huddled in a corner. "Where's Gil?" he kept asking, tears streaming down his face. The child looked up at Erak. "Daddy, I want to go home."